TWO BLACKBIRDS

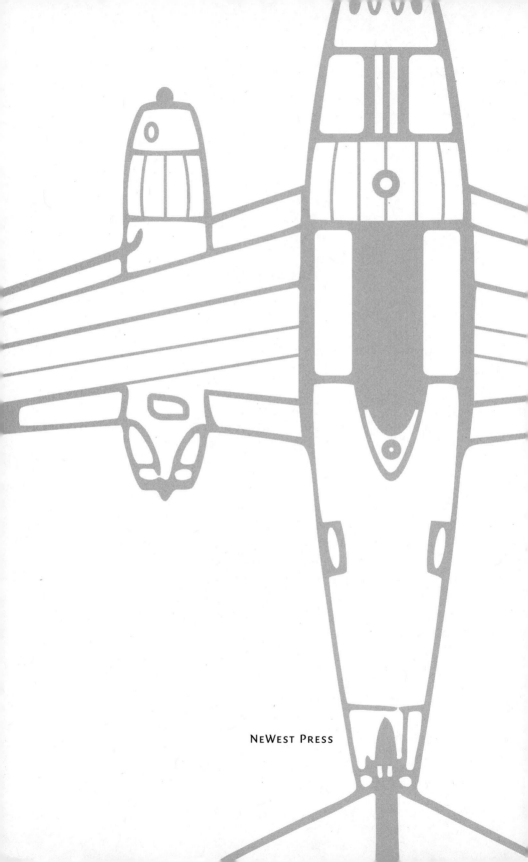

NeWest Press

A NOVEL

TWO
Blackbirds
GARRY
RYAN

COPYRIGHT ⓒ GARRY RYAN 2014

LIBRARY AND ARCHIVES CANADA CATALOGUING IN PUBLICATION
Ryan, Garry, 1953–, author
Two blackbirds / Garry Ryan.

Issued in print and electronic formats. ISBN 978-1-927063-50-7 (pbk.). — ISBN 978-1-927063-51-4 (epub). — ISBN 978-1-927063-56-9 (mobi)

I. Title.

PS8635.Y354T86 2014   c813'.6   C2013-907185-7
                                                C2013-907186-5

Editor for the Board: Jenna Butler
Cover and interior design: Natalie Olsen, Kisscut Design
Cover photography: © Peter Gudella/Shutterstock.com and Piotr Krzeslak/Shutterstock.com
Author photo: Ben Ryan

First Edition: April 2014

NeWest Press acknowledges the support of the Canada Council for the Arts, the Alberta Foundation for the Arts, and the Edmonton Arts Council for support of our publishing program. We acknowledge the financial support of the Government of Canada through the Canada Book Fund for our publishing activities.

NeWest Press

#201, 8540–109 Street
Edmonton, Alberta T6G 1E6
780.432.9427
www.newestpress.com

No bison were harmed in the making of this book.

Printed and bound in Canada by Gauvin Press

for

Walter Stuckart, who served in WWII *and came back to tell the
story of a man who was murdered in Darlington,* UK.

*Ernie Ryan, who enlisted but didn't see action,
because the atomic bombs dropped.*

*Meron Chorny, Lancaster navigator and university professor,
who taught us that "Bullshit baffles brains."*

*L-104580 Private Leslie Carr, who was killed in
Italy in 1944 and is buried at Italy's Gradara War Cemetery.
His sister Elaine never forgot him.*

*Mafalda and Ernesto Stamile. He was a soldier in Italy's army.
He taught me that "The wine is the life."
She taught me how to laugh and to swear in Spanish and Italian.*

*Hedi and Cas Kowalewski.
She said "During the war you didn't know if you'd
be alive or dead from one minute to the next."*

The red-winged blackbird
of the Canadian
prairie is
unremarkable in
size and the female is   .
unremarkable in colour.
Little larger
than a sparrow, the more skilled flyers
of this species
will drive away intruders many
times their own size.
In fact,
blackbirds have been
known to perch between the
wings of an airborne hawk or crow,
and peck on the
head of the predator
until it
withdraws.

CHAPTER 1
[TUESDAY, JUNE 13, 1944]

"What's that noise?" Sharon stepped out of the hangar and away from the mélange of oil, grease, petrol, and paint. She inhaled the fresh air, felt the sun on her face, shaded her eyes, and looked east. *It sounds like an airplane, but different,* she thought as she used her free hand to pull her non-regulation ponytail out over the collar of her blue battledress jacket.

Edgar Washington joined her. He was a bronze mountain of a man. The shovel looked like a child's beach toy in his hands. He leaned it against the wall of the hangar and looked in the direction of the noise.

They stood in the mouth of the White Waltham hangar to get a better look.

About ten feet in front of her, a wrench skidded along the concrete. "Goddamned British spanners are as useless as tits on a boar!"

"Can you hear that?" Sharon looked inside at Ernie.

"What the hell is it?" Ernie Shane stepped out of the hangar. He wore the sleeves of his dusty coveralls rolled up to reveal his Popeye arms. Ernie had a long, powerful body, short legs, and brown eyes that faced Edgar's chest whenever he looked straight ahead.

"There!" Sharon pointed south and east. The aircraft was grey, flying at a bit over two thousand feet.

"It's fast." Edgar looked over his shoulder toward London.

"Sounds like someone with the green apple quick step shitting into a forty-five-gallon drum," Ernie said.

Edgar frowned.

"It's got an odd silhouette. It looks like the engine is mounted near the tail." Sharon shaded her blue eyes with her right hand.

"It looks awfully small for an airplane," Ernie said.

"It must be some kind of jet propulsion engine," Edgar said.

Ernie nodded. "I've heard of that. Never seen one, though."

They walked around the other side of the hangar to keep their eyes on the aircraft. Sharon stood in between Edgar and Ernie. She was shorter than either of the men, but their posture revealed that they deferred to her.

The aircraft's engine stopped and it nosed down.

"Get down!" Edgar grabbed them both, pushed them to the ground, then covered their bodies with his.

"What in Christ's name are you doing?" Ernie huffed.

The answer was an explosion. The ground heaved. There was a whistling sound. When they got up and brushed themselves off, there was a piece of shrapnel the size of a dinner plate stuck in the hangar wall. It sizzled in the wood about four feet from ground level.

Ernie looked at the ragged chunk of metal, then at Edgar. "How did you know?"

Edgar shrugged. "It was coming from the direction of France, headed toward London, and it wasn't one of ours. A reasonable conclusion."

Sharon looked at the piece of shrapnel and checked to see if any of them had been wounded. "Thank you very much, Edgar." She picked dry grass from her disheveled brown hair.

Ernie slapped Edgar on the back. "I owe you one."

Edgar blushed.

"Let me buy you boys some lunch." *This is the perfect opportunity to ask Ernie for the favour,* Sharon thought.

Lunch today was courtesy of the grey NAAFI wagon, which supplied them with coffee, thick ham and cheese sandwiches, and tweed squares. They sat together at a table under a tree.

Ernie wolfed down the first half of the sandwich. "This is a nice change. It actually tastes like meat."

Edgar tucked the napkin that he kept in his back pocket into the collar of his shirt and bit into the sandwich. "The U-boats aren't sinking as many supply ships anymore, so the food's getting better."

"How come you know so much about everything?" Ernie looked sideways at Edgar.

"I read, then I look for evidence to support what I read. Last month, I read an article that said the Allies have turned the tide in the Atlantic. That U-boats were being sunk in large numbers." Edgar held up his sandwich. "You may be holding the proof in your hand."

Sharon smiled as she bit into the sandwich. *I've come to enjoy the company of men. Some of the women I work with are members of a superior class. They look down on the bastard Canadian who gives them orders. These two men don't see me that way at all.*

"I hope you're right." Ernie took a sip of coffee. "If I never taste mutton or bully beef again, it'll be too soon."

"Now we have to wait and see if the invasion is going as well as *Stars and Stripes* says it is." Edgar took a delicate bite of sandwich.

"Then the explosion this morning could be proof things are going well, or it could mean the opposite," Sharon said.

Edgar nodded. "Exactly." He glanced at Sharon with his brown eyes, then looked away. "How is Michael?"

Sharon shrugged. "I don't know. Haven't seen him for three months. After the invasion began, I finally understood why he's been so busy. He must have been working with the French Underground to prepare for the invasion. I suppose they'll be doing what they can to disrupt the Nazi supply lines."

Ernie stuffed the last of his sandwich into his mouth. He looked at Edgar before he covered his mouth with his hand and turned to Sharon. "Why not get to the point?"

Sharon smiled and set her sandwich down on the wax paper it came wrapped in. "Edgar would like to join the 332nd in Italy. He thinks that if he could be trained as an aircraft mechanic, the transfer would happen."

"332nd?" Ernie looked for a patch of clean sleeve before he wiped his mouth.

"Tuskegee Air Group. The Red Tails in Italy. It's made up of people like me."

A thoughtful frown formed on Ernie's face. He turned to Sharon. "You want me to train him?"

Sharon nodded. "That's right. You need the help. Edgar needs the training."

Ernie looked at the hangar, then at Edgar. "When do you start?"

Wrinkles appeared on Edgar's forehead when he looked at Sharon.

"I have to clear it with Edgar's CO." Sharon picked up her sandwich. "I'll phone him right after I finish this."

"Maybe not," announced a voice from behind her.

She turned.

Michael stood a head taller than her. He studied her with striking blue eyes framed by strawberry blond hair. "I hear you've had a surprise attack this morning. Thought I'd come and investigate. Apparently you've seen one of Hitler's so-called vengeance weapons."

"I wonder who his target was?" Edgar said. "His vengeance weapon crashed in an empty field. Apparently they have some problems to solve if they want to hit military targets."

"Or maybe he's declared war on cows. The only casualty was an unlucky black Angus," Ernie said.

Sharon stood and embraced her husband. She inhaled the scent of cigarettes and chocolate.

"Is the coffee any good?" Michael asked.

"Not bad." Ernie lifted his cup. "Sharon will get you a cup."

Sharon's face turned red. "He can get his own damned coffee!" She turned to her husband. "Where the hell have you been?"

"Planning an invasion," Michael said.

"I've been so worried. I thought you might have gone back into France." Sharon looked him over, checking for evidence of wounds.

"You told me not to lie to you. I couldn't very well call you up and tell you what I was up to, now could I?" Michael chuckled.

"Don't laugh at me!" Sharon said.

"It's just that you're an ace. It's not as if you haven't taken a risk or two in this war." Michael winked.

Ernie lifted his chin and looked at Edgar.

Edgar said, "So, the rumours are facts. Exactly how many aircraft have you downed?"

"Nine. I saw one crash with my own eyes." Michael looked at Edgar. "I don't believe we've been introduced." Michael offered his hand. It was dwarfed by Edgar's.

"An ace." Ernie stood up and looked at Sharon. "You never talk about it." He offered his hand to Michael. "I'm Ernie."

"Michael. Glad to meet you. You must know by now. The people who do the actual fighting in a war are often the least willing to talk about it." Michael put his arm around his wife's shoulder and pulled her closer.

CHAPTER 2
[WEDNESDAY, JUNE 14, 1944]

Linda sat at the kitchen table in the cottage that her aunt had loaned them for the duration of the war. "I made coffee." She wore her red hair cut short and had on a flight suit despite the summer heat. After being burned in a crash, she kept as much of her body covered as possible whenever she flew.

Sharon sat down across from her friend and sister-in-law. She stared at the coffee Linda had poured for her. "Thank you."

"Michael getting up?" Linda asked.

"He's asleep."

Linda smiled before she sipped. "Did you let him get any sleep at all last night?"

Sharon blushed. "Well, it has been a couple of months since I've seen him."

"You two made it difficult to sleep. Just when I was ready to nod off, you'd start up again." Linda tried to hide her smile behind her coffee cup.

Sharon thought, *You're making a joke, but you're really upset with me. You've been that way ever since the crash.*

"It's the war. You never know if this time will be the last time." Linda sipped her coffee. "You know, live for the moment because who the hell knows if you'll be alive or dead from one minute to the next. I heard about yesterday's bomb."

When you don't know what to say to Linda, change the subject. "I've got a lot of work to do today."

"So that's it, then? Wear my poor brother out and get back to work?" Linda smiled at her joke.

Sharon shook her head. "There may be a way to get us another good aircraft mechanic. I've got a call in to Edgar's commanding officer, Colonel Wright."

"You must be joking. The only reason you were able to get Ernie was because he opened his gob at the wrong time and in the wrong place to one of his superiors. There's no way you'll be able to get another one. They're like gold these days." Linda stood up and reached for her bag.

"I'll let you know later if my plan works." Sharon got up, straightened her tie and put on her blue battledress jacket.

"Ever since they made you senior commandant at White Waltham, you've become a woman possessed when it comes to safety." Linda put her cup in the sink.

Sharon did the same. "I don't want to watch another Anson crash and burn at the end of the runway because a drunken sod of a hungover mechanic forgot to tighten a fuel line." She walked to the door, stuck her feet in her shoes and leaned to tie the laces.

"Do you get a chance to fly anymore?" Linda asked.

"There are always chances to fly."

"Aren't you going to wake Michael?" Linda already had her shoes on and stood waiting.

"The war can do without him for a little while. He needs some rest. Besides, if this war has taught me one thing, it's that we're all replaceable." Sharon stood, opened the door and walked out into the morning.

The air smelled of dew. It sparkled on the grass and leaves as they walked to White Waltham.

"Mother wrote me a letter," Linda said.

"What did she have to say?" Sharon watched a pair of blackbirds dart and turn across the road.

"All is well. Sean is still being quiet, but she says that's normal.

Michael was the same way at fifteen." Linda pulled the letter from her pocket and handed it to her sister-in-law.

Sharon took the letter and stuffed it in her breast pocket. "Thanks."

He wore a white GI's helmet with MP stamped front and centre in black letters. There was a black armband on his left arm with the letters MP in white. At his hip, he wore a Colt .45 sidearm. There was a white belt across the middle of his GI service coat. "Sergeant Edwin Beck. Colonel Wilson asked me to deliver this to you."

Sharon noticed that the sergeant didn't get out of the Jeep and did not salute her — even though she was his superior officer — as he handed her the envelope. Edgar watched from the back seat where he'd crammed himself into the Jeep. She tore the end off the envelope and pulled out the letter.

ATTENTION: SENIOR COMMANDANT SHARON LACEY-TOWNSEND,

MY ADJUTANT FORWARDED YOUR REQUEST FOR EDGAR WASHINGTON TO BE REASSIGNED TO WORK WITH YOUR AIRCRAFT MECHANIC AT WHITE WALTHAM.

WASHINGTON IS YOURS TO DO WITH AS YOU SEE FIT.

ON A PERSONAL NOTE, BE ADVISED THAT YOU SHOULD WATCH WASHINGTON CLOSELY. YOU ARE AWARE OF COURSE THAT HE WAS ASSIGNED TO YOUR BASE BECAUSE SUITABLE DUTIES COULD NOT BE FOUND FOR HIM AT MINE.

SINCERELY,
COLONEL WILSON

Sharon folded the letter. "Thank you, Sergeant."

Edgar climbed out from the back seat of the Jeep.

Sergeant Beck started the Jeep. "He's all yours." He revved the engine and popped the clutch, spattering them with gravel. He shifted into top gear by the time the Jeep hit the road. He braked hard at the intersection where a rock wall marked the three-way intersection. The Jeep skidded, then fishtailed as the sergeant turned left.

"Thank you," Edgar said.

"I hope this won't make things difficult for you, Edgar."

"No more than what's usual for a man like me who wants to better himself, or a woman who likes to fly."

"Well, I'll give you that. We'd better go let Ernie know he's got some help." She walked beside Edgar to the hangar.

They found Ernie changing the magneto on an Anson's engine. "Christ in heaven, who designed this ugly son of a bitch of an aircraft?"

Edgar made a fist of his right hand, brought it to his lips and coughed.

Ernie leaned out of the engine and spied Sharon. "Ummm, good morning."

"Edgar's CO has okayed his working with you," Sharon said.

Ernie frowned.

Think fast. "I was thinking perhaps we should have a week's trial period. If either you or Edgar aren't happy with the arrangement after a week, then all one of you has to do is say so, and we go back to the way things were." Sharon looked at Ernie and at Edgar. "All right?"

Edgar nodded.

"Okay by me," Ernie said.

"Edgar, you must speak up," Sharon said.

"Sounds all right," Edgar said.

"Okay, then. I'm off to do a delivery." Sharon turned and walked out the hangar door.

"There is one thing," Edgar said.

Sharon stopped. "What?"

"I've been thinking about the flying bomb we saw yesterday. It would require some kind of internal gyroscopic control system to keep it flying straight and level. That would make it vulnerable."

Sharon faced him. "Go on."

"It might be easy to upset the flying bomb by getting a wingtip under one of its wings and flipping it over." Edgar used his hands to illustrate. "That would most likely upset the guidance system and cause it to crash."

"So a pilot would need to fly close formation and lift the flying bomb's wing?" Sharon looked at Edgar to ensure that she understood the technique.

"Yes. At first, I considered using the turbulence of an aircraft to upset the flying bomb's control system, but that would take an aircraft the size of a Lancaster bomber. We both know the bomber does not have the speed to catch the flying bomb." Edgar frowned, and the lines across his forehead became furrows. "You understand that my theory would need to be tested in the field?"

"Sounds nuts," Ernie said.

Sharon thought, *Just crazy enough that it might work.*

After a fifteen-mile ride in the Anson, Sharon was dropped off at Hawker's Langley factory at Slough. It was a massive, white-roofed facility between White Waltham and London.

A red-nosed Hawker Tempest waited in its grey and green camouflage. A fitter stood near the massive fighter with its four-blade propeller and 2,200-horsepower Sabre engine.

The fitter wore a leather vest and a wool cap. He stood on the wing root and kept one hand on the rim of the cockpit while offering Sharon his hand to lift her up off the ground. "Have you flown one these tricky bastards yet?"

Sharon nodded. "Once or twice." She took his hand, stuck her foot in the stirrup and stepped up onto the wing. "Thank you."

He waited while she climbed into the cockpit and got herself strapped in.

Sharon could feel him watching over her shoulder while she checked flaps and hydraulics before the start up.

She looked over her shoulder and smiled. "Clear!"

The fitter dropped down off the wing as she prepared to start the engine.

The propeller swung, the engine caught, and black smoke puffed from the exhaust. The air was momentarily filled up with the stink of raw gasoline. The engine smoothed itself out, and the prop wash blew the stink away.

She checked controls, instruments, and gauges before waving the wheel chocks away.

Within five minutes, she was off the ground and heading south to a new airfield at Newchurch.

She climbed to seven thousand feet, skirted the west side of London, then headed south and east to the coast. As she approached the English Channel and could see the French coast in the distance, she looked down at the emerald and olive green farm fields spread out below.

Sharon looked ahead at the coast of occupied France and remembered her nocturnal flight to pick up Michael. She looked behind the trailing edge of the wing to her right and spotted the airfield. Sharon reached for the throttle.

She took a last look around and saw an aircraft below, headed in the opposite direction. Her fighting instincts kicked in. She dipped her right wing to get a better look at it. It was the shape of a bullet with stubby wings and an engine on its back.

"Shit!" Sharon rolled the Tempest onto its back. For a moment, she hung by her harness. The webbing bit into her shoulders. She pulled back on the stick and felt the familiar, nauseating effects of the g-forces. As the plane went into a near-vertical dive, the wind screamed past the bubble canopy.

Sharon checked the airspeed indicator and found herself doing four hundred and fifty miles per hour. She leveled out, and the g-forces sucked her back down into the seat. Through a momentary haze from the sharp pullout, she saw the flying bomb ahead. She caught a whiff of the jet engine's kerosene exhaust trail when she closed within one hundred yards.

She throttled back so as not to overshoot the green and grey craft. Edgar's words came back to her: "It might be easy to upset the flying bomb by getting a wingtip under one of its wings and flipping it over."

From the rear, she got a close look at the glowing engine mounted atop the green fuselage and tail fin.

She worked the throttle and rudder to move the Tempest alongside the flying bomb. The Tempest's left wingtip tucked itself under the right wing of the unmanned craft. Sharon used the stick to lift the Tempest's left wing.

There was a thump. The stick momentarily fought her control. She brought the Tempest around in a steep turn. She twisted her neck and looked to the right. The flying bomb was nose down. It hit a field near a road. She caught the flash of the explosion and saw debris launched into the air. The Tempest bucked as it was bumped by the resulting concussion.

Sharon looked to her right and saw the Newchurch runway. *Oh, shit. They've seen what just happened. Now there will be questions. I'm sick of their damned questions about women! Like, "How can the fairer sex manage to fly combat aircraft?"*

She throttled back, checked for other aircraft, entered the circuit, did her landing checks, dropped the gear and flaps, then landed. Sharon taxied over to one of the blister hangars; it looked like someone had set a large food can on its side, dug one half into the ground, and parked aircraft inside.

In the fresh quiet following shutdown, Sharon checked to make sure the switches were off, undid her harness, climbed out, and jumped down off the trailing edge of the wing.

She took off her flying helmet, adjusted her ponytail, and looked east. A pair of fire tenders was pouring water onto a cottage. "Oh no!"

"Don't you worry. That flying bomb didn't hurt anyone. No one's moved into that cottage yet."

Sharon looked at the man behind the voice. He wore a uniform jacket. His hands were stuffed into his pockets. "Gerard." He pulled his right hand out and offered it to Sharon.

She took the hand. "Sharon."

"I didn't hear any cannon fire. What exactly did you do to make that doodlebug crash?" Gerard asked.

"Is that what those things are called?" *He's talking to you pilot to pilot. It's okay. Just answer the question.*

"That's what *I* call them. Well, how did you do it?"

"A friend told me that it had to have some kind of internal gyro to keep it flying straight and level. He said that if I flew alongside and used my wingtip to flip its wing —" She used her hands to illustrate the maneuver. "— it would cause the doodlebug to crash. This Tempest has no ammunition, so I decided to try it."

"It certainly appears to have worked. I'll have to give it a try; after all, we've been moved down here to intercept those bastards before they can reach London." Gerard looked at the NAAFI wagon parked across the field at the dispersal hut. "Mind if I give you a lift? I was planning to get a cuppa." He moved toward a Jeep parked nearby.

"How did you manage to get one of these?" Sharon admired the Jeep as she set her parachute and helmet behind the seat.

"That's a long story," Gerard said. "Some very nice Americans lent it to me. I'll bet you didn't know that these things tip over easily."

There was a popping sound. The flare of a white Very light left a smoky trail in the sky. It reached the top of its arc, then began to fall down. A pair of Tempests started up. Gerard waited as the pair took off in a roar that made conversation difficult. The fighters headed west.

"It appears that I'll have to drop you at the NAAFI van. Something's up. I need to check in." Gerard started the Jeep.

Later, while she sipped coffee and waited for a ride in the air taxi, Sharon reached into her pocket and pulled out Honeysuckle's letter.

JUNE 7, 1944

DEAR LINDA AND SHARON,

THE DAYS HAVE BEEN GLORIOUS HERE. EVERYTHING IS ALIVE, RIPE, AND GROWING AT AN INCREDIBLE PACE. THAT INCLUDES SEAN, OF COURSE, WHO CONTINUES TO READ THE NEWSPAPER AND LISTEN TO THE RADIO FOR ANY NEWS OF HIS BIG SISTER, AUNT, AND UNCLE. AS ALWAYS, THE HEROES HE HEARS ABOUT ARE NOT THE THREE OF YOU. BY THE WAY, HIS HEALTHY APPETITE HAS RESULTED IN HIS GROWING TALLER AND MY PUTTING ON A FEW EXTRA POUNDS. I DON'T KNOW WHY I THINK I HAVE TO KEEP UP WITH HIM.

AT LEAST NOW WE KNOW WHY WE'VE HEARD AND SEEN SO LITTLE FROM MICHAEL AND HARRY. THE INVASION IS ON, AND THE PAIR OF THEM MUST BE IN THE THICK OF THE PLANNING. I HOPE THIS DREARY OLD WAR WILL BE OVER BY CHRISTMAS.

I HEAR THAT CORNELIA IS WELL AND HAS BEEN SEEN OUT AND ABOUT.

IT WOULD BE GOOD IF BOTH OF YOU COULD MAKE A TRIP NORTH THIS MONTH OR NEXT. SEAN HAS BEGUN TO SPEND TOO MUCH TIME ALONE. OF COURSE, HE HELPS OUT WITH THE FARM, AND HE IS ALWAYS PLEASANT WITH ME. THE REASON FOR HIS RETICENCE, I BELIEVE, IS THE APPROACHING FOURTH ANNIVERSARY OF HIS PARENTS' DEATHS. I CANNOT PUT MY CONCERN INTO WORDS EXACTLY, BUT I FEAR HE IS MORE TROUBLED BY THE APPROACH OF THIS AUGUST EIGHTEENTH THAN ANY OF THE OTHERS.

AS ALWAYS, WE SEND OUR LOVE TO YOU.

SINCERELY,
HONEYSUCKLE

"How was the trip to Newcastle?" Mother asked as Sharon entered the dusty dispersal hut at White Waltham. A fresh haircut made him look younger and less harried than he'd appeared during the delivery mayhem leading up to the invasion. He'd even had the barber trim the grey eyebrows that had grown into a thicket above his eyes. (Mother's real name was Mr. Green. His nickname was in recognition of the motherly concern he displayed for the pilots under his care.)

"Fine. You look younger, Mother." Sharon looked around the room to see that they were alone. "Everyone's off on deliveries, I see."

"Care to fill in the details about the flight to Newcastle? You see, I have a friend who works there now." Mother crossed his arms and leaned his back against the wall. "Communications have vastly improved since the beginning of the war."

"Only one friend? You have connections all over this island. And it appears you already know what happened, so why don't you tell me what you've heard?" Sharon set her parachute on a table and sat down.

"Apparently, you put on an aerial demonstration. The lesson was how to down a flying bomb without firing a shot." Mother scratched his cheek, discovered a spot he'd missed after this morning's shave, and frowned.

"Unfortunately, it was also a lesson on how to destroy an uninhabited cottage." Sharon looked out the open door. She could see the hangar from here. "I wonder how Edgar and Ernie are getting along?"

"A cottage? It's quite an accomplishment to hit anything other than an open field in Newchurch. It must be the only location in the British Isles with fewer people per square mile than Canada." Mother looked sideways at Sharon.

"Really?" she smiled.

Mother nodded. "Really."

"How difficult would it be for Linda and me to get a delivery to Leeds before the end of the week? I think it's time the two of us went home for forty-eight hours." Sharon looked out the door again in case Ernie was throwing something or someone out of — or worse, through — the hangar door.

"Shouldn't be a problem. And don't be worrying yourself about those two misfits. Haven't seen or heard anything from Ernie or Edgar at all today." Mother nodded in the direction of the hangar.

"Well, I need to thank one of those misfits. Edgar was the one who told me how to send that flying bomb diving into the ground. It worked like a charm." Sharon stood up and walked out the door of the dispersal hut. She made her way to the hangar and waited just outside of the open door.

"Shit!" Ernie said.

"I only said that if the design of this oleo leg was modified by six degrees, the entire assembly would become much more durable and easier to maintain," Edgar said.

"I know this damned British engineering is abominable. Every mechanic who works on this shit knows that! We just don't have the time or the equipment to do the modifications!"

Sharon stepped inside the hangar and saw the two men working on one of the wheel struts of an Anson. The aircraft had grown a little long in the tooth after four years of hauling pilots from the far corners of the island and back again. "Just stopped by to see how you're both doing."

"All right." Ernie sounded surprised.

"Edgar?" Sharon asked.

He looked over his shoulder. "Okay."

"I wanted to let you know that your tactic for upsetting a flying bomb's gyros worked perfectly."

Edgar nodded and looked at her thoughtfully. "I'm surprised you had the opportunity to test the theory so quickly."

"You never know what you'll need to know from one moment to the next in this war," she said.

CHAPTER 3
[THURSDAY, JUNE 22, 1944]

"Where did this contraption come from?" Sharon looked at the broad wings, greenhouse glass cockpit, wing struts, and tiny wheels of the captured German aircraft. "It looks like a stork with black crosses on it."

"Very close. It's actually called a Storch. Apparently, it was captured just a few days into the invasion, along with fifteen others." Mother pointed at the hastily painted black and white invasion stripes on the wings. "It was supposed to go to some Army colonel. Instead, it was sent here for evaluation. Robert did us a favour."

"Robert?"

"A friend of mine."

"Why here?" Sharon asked.

Mother shook his head and offered the phrase that explained away any inexplicable event that might occur at times like these: "There's a war on."

Ernie lifted the cowling and peered inside. "Air-cooled v8. Plenty of power for a machine this size."

Edgar ran his fingers along the trailing edge of the wing. "Looks like it could land or take off almost anywhere."

Mother scratched his chin and winked at her. "I was thinking that it might require an extended cross country flight to West Yorkshire — say, Ilkley. I would suggest that Linda fly with you so that we'll get more than one opinion as to its capabilities."

"A little bit of work needs to be done first." Ernie ticked off the tasks on his fingers. "We have to do a complete check to make sure she's airworthy. And we'll need a test flight." He winked at Edgar. "I think we'll both need a ride to make sure it's safe. Of course, some painting will need to be done." He pointed at the black crosses on the wings. "Especially there." He jerked a thumb at the swastika on the tail.

Edgar nodded. "Most definitely."

Sharon looked at each of them. "Will this evening be too early for the two of you to come along for test flights?"

"Before six?" Edgar asked.

"Edgar's ride comes at six," Ernie said.

"Okay. Before six it is." Sharon walked back to the dispersal hut with Mother. "Do you have a delivery for me?"

"A Lancaster is waiting for you at Woodford." Mother handed her a chit.

"All the way up north to Manchester. Close to home," Sharon said.

"Remember, you need to be back before six," Mother said.

"Where does the Lanc go?" Sharon asked.

Fours hours later, Sharon had four twelve-hundred-horsepower Merlin engines in her hands. She looked to port over the green-and-brown camouflaged expanse of its wing. The Lancaster was a bit of a pussy-cat when it wasn't loaded down with bombs, crew, and fuel. Sharon throttled back the four engines to join the circuit at the RAF airfield at Woodhill Spa near the east coast, north of London. She made her pre-landing checks, lowered the undercarriage, and settled the heavy bomber onto the runway.

She used throttle and idiosyncratic brakes to guide the bomber close to the apron out front of one of the massive hangars, with its green doors and white roof. The brakes moaned when she applied and locked them. It took a few minutes to shut down all four engines and work her way through the post-flight checklist. She exited through the rear door where the camouflaged top of the fuselage met the black underside of the aircraft.

"You ever wonder what happens after you deliver one of these machines?"

Sharon saw the silhouette of an unknown person inside the subdued half-light of the hangar. She hitched her parachute harness over her shoulder and walked toward the voice.

"I asked you a question."

"I know, but it's difficult to see who I'm speaking to." Sharon passed under the bomber's wing. She could smell the engine oil and feel the heat from the engines as she walked between the stationary propellers.

"Well?" The man stepped into the open. He was over six feet tall and weighed maybe one hundred and eighty pounds. His coveralls were clean and grey. His black hair was combed back. His brown eyes were red from crying and set on either side of a crooked nose.

"What's your name?" Sharon asked.

"Trevor. Now answer the question." He put his fists on his hips.

"I wonder about the crew of the bomber this Lancaster is replacing."

"They were my boys." Trevor went to say more, but took a long, shuddering breath instead. "Last night's target was Wesseling. The ones who made it back said the night fighters were thick, and so was the flak."

"I'm sorry."

"Losses were nearly thirty percent. We lost six crews. That's seven boys in each Lancaster." Trevor pulled a rag from his pocket and began to wipe at his hands.

Sharon could see that the man's hands were already clean. "Can I get you a cup of coffee?"

Trevor looked at her. "I don't want a cup of coffee. I want this fucking war to be over."

Sharon felt the familiar weariness from fighting, casualty lists, and the nagging feeling that nothing would ever be the same, even after the war ended.

It was ten after six when Sharon touched down at White Waltham. She was at the controls of the Storch. Edgar was in the rear seat.

"Amazing," Sharon said. The high-winged German aircraft landed at just under forty miles an hour and took less than seventy feet to roll to a stop. *It's better at this kind of flying than anything we have.*

She looked over her shoulder. Edgar was opening up the canopy, leaning out and throwing up along the freshly painted outer skin. Ernie and Edgar had just put black and white invasion stripes on the fuselage and tail to cover the black crosses and swastika. The wings looked like a piano keyboard.

A Jeep was parked next to hangar as she taxied over, jazzed the throttle, swung the tail around, and shut down. She opened the forward canopy and backed out. Edgar followed.

"You're late, boy." Sergeant Beck leaned against the grill of the Jeep and pointed with a lit cigarette. "That's some kinda paint job, boy!"

Sharon glared at the American MP. "His name is Edgar!"

Beck smiled back at her, leaned forward, and took a languid drag from his cigarette. "Time to get you back to the base. . . Edgar."

Edgar said nothing as he climbed into the back of the Jeep.

Sharon saw Sergeant Beck turn to say something to Edgar. As the MP turned back around to start the engine — for just a fleeting moment — she saw something in Edgar's eyes. The same something she'd seen in the mirror above a Spitfire's cockpit minutes before she shot down five aircraft and killed their crews.

Edgar held on as Beck roared away.

"That's one asshole of a Yank," Ernie said.

Sharon continued to shiver from the flashback to her own murderous impulses as she looked at the Ernie. "Now that you mention it, he does remind me of Uncle Marmaduke."

"No idea who that is. Well, what do you think of the Storch?" Ernie asked.

"Climb in, and we'll see what you think after a hop."

"Shouldn't I give it a wash first?" Ernie asked.

Sharon shook her head. "It's all on the outside. You'd think Edgar had never flown before."

"He hasn't."

"You're kidding." Sharon turned to face Ernie.

"Nope. And when are we gonna talk about whether or not Edgar is staying?"

Sharon put her flying helmet on. "When we get back."

Forty minutes later, they sat in the canteen having supper. It was ham, beans, and potatoes. Astonishingly, a slice of fresh bread was part of the meal.

Ernie watched as Sharon used bread to sop up the sauce from the beans. He asked, "How can you eat that?"

Sharon looked at him. Sauce dribbled from the corner of her mouth. She used a napkin to wipe it away. "I haven't eaten since breakfast." She looked at his plate. He hadn't touched it. "You're not feeling well?"

Ernie frowned and reached for a glass of water. He hid a belch behind his hand.

"Oh, I'm sorry. I shouldn't have done the roll and the loop." *I thought you had flown before.*

"I thought we were going to talk about Edgar." Ernie slowly sipped the water.

Okay, I get it, you want to change the subject. You're tough and you're not going to admit a weak stomach in front of a woman. "What do you think? Is he going to be a good mechanic?"

"I only have to show him once, and he remembers how to do something just the way I've taught him. He's smart, way too smart for this job. He keeps telling me how each part could be designed better, and I keep telling him we don't have time to design, we only have time to fix. It's like he sees how it should be built and then starts redesigning things in his head." Ernie pointed his index finger at his temple.

"So you're saying you don't want to work with him anymore?"

"No. You're not listening. I'm saying he's so smart, he should be designing aircraft instead of fixing them." Ernie looked at a point somewhere in the distance.

"So you want to keep working with him?"

"Of course. He's found ways to reorganize the shop and do repairs that I never would have thought of. And almost every time he comes up with an idea, it works." Ernie looked at his plate, picked up a piece of ham, and gingerly placed it in his mouth.

CHAPTER 4
[FRIDAY, JUNE 23, 1944]

Edgar stepped out of the back of the Jeep, tucked his fists against the small of his spine, leaned back, and stretched. The morning sun illuminated his face.

Beck popped the clutch and the Jeep's rear wheels spit gravel over the toes of Edgar's boots.

Sharon watched the MP race for the end of the road. The Jeep skidded as Beck slammed on the brakes and slid sideways around the corner. "One of these times, he's gonna hit that wall. Would you like a coffee?" She held a cup out with her left hand while sipping from the one in her right.

"I thought we were supposed to get our own damned coffee." Edgar smiled and looked at the cup as if expecting some kind of trap.

Sharon gestured with the cup. "This may never happen again, so I'd take advantage of it."

Edgar took the cup, took a sip, and closed his eyes. "Thank you."

"I need to ask you if you want to keep working here."

Edgar opened his eyes and studied Sharon. "What does that mean, exactly?"

"I said I would talk to you and see if you would agree to keep working here. It's been more than a week, and here we are." Sharon watched Edgar. "Are you happy here?"

"Except for the driver and Ernie's profanity, yes, I am." Edgar took another sip of coffee.

"His swearing offends you?" Sharon asked.

"He uses the Lord's name in vain."

"He does. That's for sure. He also speaks highly of you."

"He does?"

Sharon nodded. "He does."

"You're asking me if I want to stay?"

"That's right." *Maybe I'm missing the point. Maybe he's not used to being asked.*

"Yes, I would like to stay." Edgar nodded.

"Glad to have you, then."

Edgar's smile lit up the morning.

CHAPTER 5

[SATURDAY, JUNE 24, 1944]

The deuce and a half had white stars painted on its olive green doors and hood, and a canvas cover over its rear deck. The two-and-a-half-ton truck rolled up next to the hangar door.

Sharon watched from the rear seat of the Storch while Linda went through the preflight checks.

The driver stepped down from the truck. "Where's my high yellow friend?"

Ernie leaned back and peered out from the guts of an engine he'd pulled from an Anson. "Who the hell you lookin' for?"

"My high yellow friend." The driver removed his cap. He was about five foot ten, weighed maybe one hundred and forty pounds, and had close-cut, tightly curled black hair.

"What the hell are you talkin' about?" Ernie asked.

"Cream in your coffee." The driver pointed at his chest. "I'm black coffee. Edgar is high yellow."

"Edgar? Why the hell didn't you say so?" Ernie pointed to the back of the hangar.

Edgar hauled a jack stand from the rear of the building. He looked up. "Walter?"

"Of course it's me! Be quick now! We gotta unload this, and I gotta get back to the base, or people'll start askin' questions." Walter smiled as Edgar dropped the jack stand with a clang and ran over to the truck.

Edgar said, "Come on, Ernie!"

The three men began to unload boxes from the back of the truck.

"What the hell is this stuff?" Ernie asked.

"Keep your voice down. It's new tools." Edgar looked in Sharon's direction before grabbing one end of the largest box and sliding it partway off the truck.

Ernie grabbed the other end. They hefted the load into the hangar. Both made hasty glances in Sharon's direction. She waved. *We could sure use a better set of tools. Ernie is always asking, I'm always filling out requisitions and it never happens. So Edgar delivers.*

Walter climbed into the cab of the truck and started the engine.

"Clear!" Linda said. The Storch's propeller turned and the engine caught.

The flight was uneventful until they were less than an hour from their destination — Townsend Farm in the northwest of Britain. Sharon was flying this leg of the trip and sat in the front seat. Linda tapped her on the shoulder. Sharon turned to see that Linda was gesturing to their right.

A Spitfire flew past, followed by his wingman. Both aircraft waggled their wings and turned to the left.

Sharon instinctively reached for the throttle. *If I slow down, they won't be able to fly alongside us; they'll fall out of the sky first.* She eased off the throttle and dropped some flap. The Storch was quite happy flying at forty miles per hour — probably thirty miles per hour slower than the stalling speed of the Spitfires. "Keep your eyes open and let me know if they're making another pass!"

"You think they'll shoot?" Linda asked.

Crazier things have happened. Sharon shoulder checked, then turned right, keeping an eye on the fighters as they swung around. She leveled out and approached the fighters head on. Before they came in range, she turned again, then shoved the nose of the aircraft toward the ground.

The Storch was incredibly maneuverable at low speed. The faster fighters could not follow it in a turn. The lead Spitfire fired a short burst. The tracers from the cannon shells went high and wide.

The Spitfire pilots tried two more passes. Each time, Sharon kept her flying speed low and turned inside of them. *If you have to, you can drop down to one hundred feet.* Then she thought, *No. One of them will make a mistake, stall, and crash. Just keep your cool. No need to get anyone killed.*

The Spitfires made another pass. This time, the wingman dropped his flaps and undercarriage, flew alongside, and pointed at them to follow. For an instant, Sharon saw a look of surprise on the pilot's face. *We can't do this all day.* Sharon opened the throttle, lifted the flaps, and was just able to keep up with the Spitfire, which was flying just above its stalling speed as it led the way to Barton Airfield near Manchester.

She said to Linda, "Keep an eye on the other Spit in case this is a trick."

The other Spitfire circled overhead just to be certain Sharon did as she was directed.

Sharon followed the slow-flying Spitfire as it passed over a line of railway tracks. When she saw Barton Airfield, Sharon pointed the Storch's nose at the hangar, throttled back, dropped the flaps, and landed just in front of it.

The Spitfires landed one after the other and taxied near to the Storch. Sharon and Linda climbed out of the plane, stood beside it, and waited.

Linda pointed at the lead aircraft. There were holes in the yellow patches of tape covering its machine guns. Its pilot climbed out, jumped off the wing, and took off his parachute and helmet before walking toward them. Behind him, the second pilot ran to catch up.

The first pilot stopped in front them and put his hands on his hips. "What the hell do the two of you think you're doing?" He was a little over five feet, weighed maybe one hundred and thirty pounds, and wore his brown hair slicked back. His accent was Canadian.

"An authorized evaluation of a captured aircraft. Did you happen to notice the way the entire aircraft is painted with white and black stripes?" *Just give him a chance to cool down.*

The second pilot was almost there.

Linda said, "What makes you think you were justified in shooting at us? Couldn't you see that we're unarmed and painted in invasion colours? In fact —" She pointed at the Spitfires. "— you have the same black and white stripes on the wings of your aircraft."

The first pilot said, "I don't have to justify myself to you!"

You shouldn't have used such a patronizing tone with Linda.

Sure enough, Linda took a step forward, cocked her arm, and punched him in the nose. The injured pilot staggered back with his hands cupped over his face. He bent at the waist. The blood dripped through his fingers. He looked up at Linda with a combination of shock and rage.

The second pilot was breathless when he arrived. He pulled off his flying helmet to reveal curly black hair plastered to his scalp. He wiped his forehead with the inside of his elbow and studied Linda with his dark brown eyes.

Sharon took Linda's elbow and walked her friend toward the hangar. "I hate it when they talk to me like that," Linda said. "I bet I've got more hours in the air than the pair of them put together!"

"And the really amazing thing was that the other pilot — the handsome one — was smitten with Linda!" Sharon slapped her hand on the table in the garden at Honeysuckle's home. The roses were in full bloom and filled the air with their scent.

"No, he wasn't," Linda said, a little too quickly. Her face turned red.

"What was his name?" Honeysuckle wore her hair shorter now after a disastrous haircut and colour. Two months ago, her hair was jet black. Today, there was a grey stripe over the top of her head with black all around the edges. She'd vowed to let the colour grow out and usually wore a dilapidated, hand-me-down tweed trilby to cover up the mess.

"Myron or Meron or. . ." Sharon frowned.

"Milton," Linda said.

"So you did notice!" Honeysuckle said.

"Oh, shut up." Linda reached for a sandwich.

"I think it's because you punched the other pilot in the nose. I got the distinct impression that you did what Milton was dying to do. After all, Milton was the civilized one."

"Tell me you didn't punch the other pilot," Honeysuckle said.

"He was the idiot who opened fire on us. Of course, Sharon had already anticipated his next move, and we were never in harm's way," Linda added quickly, anticipating her mother's reaction to the news.

"Someone was shooting at you?" Honeysuckle asked.

"Yes." Sharon put her hand on Honeysuckle's shoulder. "We're flying a captured German aircraft. Linda spotted the Spitfires before we were in any real danger. The first pilot was a trigger-happy Canadian. Luckily, Milton was smarter and dropped his flaps and wheels, then led us into Barton. It's less than an hour southwest of here."

Linda got up and stood next to her mother. "The Storch is painted black and white all over. The stupid bastard in the lead airplane wasn't paying attention. He was just looking to put a notch in his gun belt."

Honeysuckle shook her head. "Did you break his nose?"

"I hope so," Linda said.

"Where's Sean?" Sharon asked.

"I've been wondering that, too," Linda said.

"He went for a walk with Sam." Honeysuckle smiled.

"Sam?" Linda asked.

"Oh, I didn't tell you. We have a new dog named Sam — a cross between something and something else. He's only three months old, and the two of them are becoming quite close." Honeysuckle sat up and looked over her shoulder. "They like to go for long walks. Sean is trying to train Sam. Without much success, I might add."

Sharon stood up. "Which direction?"

Honeysuckle pointed east along a familiar pathway.

"I'll see if I can find them." Sharon stood up and walked down through a gap in the trees.

The pathway meandered around the trunks of evergreen and birch trees. Bluebells covered the ground on either side of the pathway. She felt a longing for home and the western slopes of the Canadian Rockies where trees grew all the way up to the mountains' shoulders.

The trees thinned to reveal a pasture framed on all four sides by a rock wall. She could see Sean leaning with his back against the east wall and his face to the sun. His legs were stretched out and his feet at awkward angles. A brown, black, and white dog lay with its chin on his lap.

Sharon walked closer. The knee-high grass brushed against her trousers.

The dog's head lifted. Sean kept his eyes closed as he rubbed Sam's head.

Sharon slowed her steps. Sam's tail wagged once. Sharon put her finger to her lips. Sam barked.

Sean's eyes opened. He smiled at his sister, then wiped the drool away from his chin.

Sharon reached out with her right hand. He grabbed it, and she pulled him to his feet.

"You've grown another foot." Sharon had to look up to meet his gaze.

Sean patted her on the top of the head. They shared the same shade of brown in their hair. Their eyes were blue. His shoulders were broader now, and he had a barrel chest. "I didn't hear you arrive. Did you fly in?"

She nodded as she took him in. "Your voice is changing." *You sound just like our father. I can see Patrick in front of the hangar just before he was killed.*

Sam stretched his paws out front, lowered his head, curled his tail, and yawned.

"Why are you crying?" Sean asked.

"You sound just like Patrick." Sharon wiped a sleeve across her eyes.

"Really?" he asked.

"Really," Sharon nodded. "And you look like him, too."

"I can't remember what he or my mother looked like. It's been almost four years since they were killed."

"Look in the mirror and you'll see Dad," Sharon said.

"So, what do I do about my mom? There weren't any pictures left in the rubble, were there?" Sean began to walk in the direction of Honeysuckle's home.

"Is right after supper okay?" Sharon looked at Honeysuckle.

"Perhaps before would be better," Honeysuckle said.

Sharon frowned, saw Honeysuckle nod in Sean's direction, and remembered Edgar's airsickness. "Of course."

Linda said, "Go on. Mother and I need to do some catching up."

Sharon grabbed her goggles and helmet. "Think there will be any trouble with trigger-happy colonials this time?"

Linda shook her head. "This is West Yorkshire. There isn't much in the way of air traffic around here. Most of that is on the east side of the country."

Sean waited for Sharon to go out the back door first. She nodded and headed out.

"I have to tie up the dog or he'll follow us." Sean whistled for Sam.

For five minutes, the dog ran in circles around them. Each time Sean or Sharon would get close, he'd dart away. Finally he tired, and Sharon grabbed him by the collar. Sean tied a leash to the dog's collar, tied the other end to a ring in the barn, and set a dish of water in front of Sam. "Now we can go."

She let Sean lead her through the preflight checks on the Storch and helped with the finer points while explaining its handling characteristics.

"Sit up front." Sharon climbed into the back seat.

She took care of the takeoff and took a good long look around for other aircraft before she said, "You have control."

Sean took a few minutes to get used to the new controls before trying a few gentle turns.

Sharon figured they'd been able to squeeze in about fifty hours of flying time over the past three years. She tapped him on the shoulder. "Do you want to try a landing?"

Sean looked back over his shoulder, smiled, and nodded. He headed for home and took a careful look at the surrounding sky before preparing to land.

On short finals, Sharon leaned her head around to the right, then did the same on the left. She saw a person walking from left to right across the field next to the Townsend Farm. The walker and the Storch were on a collision course.

She tapped Sean on the shoulder. "I have control!"

Sean lifted his hands away from the controls to show her he heard and understood.

Sharon added power and leveled out at fifty feet. She looked down to see the upturned face of a woman who looked like her grandmother. The woman's hair looked wildly unkempt. She wore a pair of Wellington boots and nothing else.

Sharon did another circuit. Cornelia had disappeared. Sharon did a short-field landing just in case Cornelia jumped out in front of them.

At supper, Sharon asked, "Have any of you seen Cornelia lately?"

Linda looked at Honeysuckle, who said, "It's something we need to talk about. Cornelia, unfortunately, has not been well."

"I saw an old woman out in the pasture. She was wearing nothing but her Wellingtons." Sharon looked at Sean, who had taken a sudden interest in looking through the kitchen window. "It looked like my grandmother."

"Most likely it was." Honeysuckle put her hand on Sharon's. "It looks like she's suffering from dementia."

"It happened suddenly?" Sharon asked.

"She hasn't been feeling well for about four months. The last two weeks have been especially difficult." Honeysuckle hesitated.

"What?" Sharon asked.

"Walter McGregor called when you and Sean were out. He asked to see you in the morning." Honeysuckle used her fork to point at Sharon and Sean.

"What about?" Sharon asked.

Honeysuckle shook her head. "He didn't say."

After supper, the cleanup, and a freshly brewed pot of tea, Honeysuckle and Linda settled into a catch-up session.

"Tell me more about this Milton," Honeysuckle said.

Linda blushed again.

Sean stood up. "Sam needs a walk."

Sharon looked at her friend.

Linda cocked her head to the left as if to say, "I can handle this; you go with Sean."

Sharon stood and patted her full stomach. "Hang on, Sean. Mind if I tag along?"

Sean stopped at the door, turned around, and smiled.

As they walked out of the door, they could hear Linda when she said, "Yes, Mom, he was very nice. But I don't think I'll be seeing him again."

Sean closed the door and went to the barn to get Sam. The dog had a bed in one of the empty stalls. Then Sam was straining at the end of his leash as he dragged Sean out of the barn. "Hold on, you daft twit!" Sean said.

Sharon grabbed Sam by the collar. "Sit!"

Sam cocked his head and gave her a puzzled look. She pushed his back end down until he assumed a posture more to her liking.

"What are you doing?" Sean asked.

"Unfortunately, dogs have a pecking order." She looked at her brother. "And it doesn't work very well when you're at the bottom of the dog's pecking order."

"A class system, then?" Sean reached for the leash.

"Something like that." Sharon walked west toward her grandmother's estate.

"You sure you want to go that way?" Sean asked.

Without turning around, Sharon asked, "Why not?"

"Your Uncle Marmaduke is a wanker, that's why." Sean pulled up beside her with the dog in between.

Sharon smiled. "So you've bumped into him?"

"More than once." Sean looked ahead to where a hedge ran along the edge of a pasture.

A woman stepped through a gap in the hedge. Her white hair was uncombed. She wore a floral print dress and Wellington boots. She lifted her dress and squatted.

"Grandmother?" Sharon caught the strong scent of urine on the breeze.

The woman looked their way. "I don't know where my friend is."

"Cornelia?" *She sounds like a child.* They were within fifteen feet of Cornelia, and Sharon saw the vagueness in her blue eyes.

Cornelia stood and let her dress fall. "Do you know where Agnes is?"

"Agnes?" Sharon asked.

"Yes, Agnes. My friend." Cornelia bent at the waist to peer around Sharon and Sean as if she might find Agnes hiding behind them. "That's a nice dog you've got."

"His name is Sam," Sean said.

"Do you want us to take you home?" Sharon asked.

"No!" Cornelia turned and walked through the gap in the hedge. Sharon followed.

Sam sniffed the pee patch. Sean pulled him away and followed his sister.

"Cornelia?" Sharon asked.

"You might want to stay on this side of the hedge," Sean said to Sharon.

"She's my grandmother." Sharon turned a branch to the side and pushed through.

In the clearing beyond the hedge, Cornelia was walking purposefully to the west.

Walking toward them was a man dressed in black hat, scarlet jacket, white jodhpurs, and black leather riding boots. Sharon recognized her Uncle Marmaduke's hooked nose.

"Now we've had it," Sean said.

Sam barked.

"Mother!" Marmaduke pointed his leather-gloved hand in the air for emphasis. "Where the hell have you been?"

"Looking for Agnes," Cornelia said.

"Agnes died ten years ago," Marmaduke said.

Cornelia began to cry. "No, she didn't. Agnes is my friend. We go to school together. She said she'd meet me down there." She pointed toward the gap in the hedge.

Marmaduke raised his hand. "You're being ridiculous."

Cornelia ducked her head.

"Hello, Uncle." Sharon felt Sean grow tense beside her.

Marmaduke stared at Sharon, then at Sean.

Sharon saw his pupils narrowing, his nostrils flaring, and his head pulling back. *He looks like a horse,* she thought, and it made her smile.

"What's so damned funny?" Marmaduke asked.

Sharon planted her feet and looked up at her uncle. "Well, you are, of course. It must be difficult for the other fox hunters to distinguish between you and your horse." *I'm not afraid of you,* she thought.

Marmaduke's eyes grew wide. He took a step forward and cocked his right arm.

Sharon moved closer to her grandmother. She sensed Sean moving closer to stand beside her. Sam strained at the leash and growled.

Marmaduke dropped his arm.

"Agnes?" Cornelia asked and walked past her son.

"You and your mongrel brother are trespassing on my land. Leave!" Marmaduke said, then turned to follow his mother.

Rage's fire lit Sharon. She stepped forward.

Sean grabbed her arm. "Let him go."

She turned to her brother, tried to reply, and found she could not.

"You know, you're absolutely right. He does look very much like a horse."

Sharon shook her head and smiled. "He does, doesn't he?"

"Let's go and see if Linda is still being interrogated by Honeysuckle." Sean pulled on the leash, tugged Sharon's elbow, and headed east.

"Do you see him around very often?" Sharon asked as she freed herself from Sean's grip.

"Every so often." Sean looked at Sam and smiled.

Ask him. "What do your friends think of him?"

"Friends?" Sean's eyes locked on hers.

"Well?" Sharon asked.

He lifted his chin in the direction of the retreating Marmaduke. "It's not a good idea for anyone around here to be my friend. Your uncle has made it clear that there will be a price to pay if anyone defies him by being seen with me. Besides, there aren't many males around here. After all, there is a war on."

"Is that why Honeysuckle decided to get Sam?" Sharon hurried to catch up with Sean, who was closing in on the gap in the hedge. He ducked his head and stepped through.

She found him waiting on the other side. "I thought you would be safe here. I thought Honeysuckle would be good to you."

"She is. There aren't many people who are willing to stand up to Marmaduke Lacey other than Honeysuckle, and for some reason, he's afraid of her."

"Michael told me something that might help you understand why he's worried."

Sean leaned to pick up a stone. He tossed it over Sam's head. The dog gave chase. Sean looked at Sharon.

"Apparently, Marmaduke was known to be associated with Oswald Mosley in the early part of the war." Sharon studied her brother's reaction to the news.

"Who's he?"

"A fascist. He thought Mussolini had the right idea about how to run a country and that England should follow suit." Sharon put her hand on Sean's shoulder. "You understand that this information is not to be shared?"

Sean nodded. "Yes. Of course. But I thought Italy surrendered. And besides, why are you telling me this?"

"It did, and Mussolini is finished. Marmaduke is afraid that people will find out he supported Mosley and Mussolini. It will make him look like a traitor to his country. So he leaves Honeysuckle alone because she might share that information with the people around here. Did you know that Townsend works for MI5?"

"You're joking! Harry? Honeysuckle's husband? He works for Intelligence?"

"So does Michael," Sharon said.

"I knew that, but Harry? He's so. . ." Sean was unable to complete the sentence.

"The polite word is 'eccentric.' And that's why Marmaduke is afraid. He thinks Harry might let it slip at the pub during one of his visits home."

Sean rubbed Sam behind the ears. "Dogs are much easier to get along with than people."

CHAPTER 6
[MONDAY, JUNE 26, 1944]

Sean drove the Austin and Sharon sat in the passenger seat. He ground a couple of teeth off third gear as he shifted up from second. Skipton Road was on the south side of the River Wharfe. The tarmac road carried them along on its back into the town of Ilkley. The Cow and Calf rocks looked down on the town from their vantage point on the hill.

Sharon looked out the window, thinking about her mother, grandmother, and father. *All three of them are gone. Well, Cornelia is still alive, but her mind is gone.*

At the edge of town, the Austin's brakes began to complain. Sharon looked ahead.

A man in a scarlet coat and white pants was perched atop a white stallion with an erection the length and girth of a baseball bat.

Sharon glanced to her right.

Sean blushed.

The rider stood up in the stirrups and blew his horn. A pack of hounds appeared, swirled around the hooves of the stallion, and disappeared into the brush on the other side of the road. More horses and riders followed. Some looked down on the Austin as they pranced across the road. Marmaduke brought up the rear, stopped in the middle of the road, looked down on them, then spurred his horse forward.

"Since you first pointed it out, I have to say that the resemblance between Marmaduke and his horse is remarkably accurate. It almost makes me think that, perhaps. . ." Sean revved the engine before releasing the clutch and jerking forward. "Sorry."

She hung on. "Don't worry. You're getting the hang of it. Do you want to finish that thought?"

He blushed. "What did your grandfather look like? And what was he up to in his stables?" He pulled up in front of a tan-coloured three-storey stone building at the centre of town.

"I thought we were going to McGregor's office," Sharon said.

"He moved when his son came back from the war." Sean shut off the engine.

"Which son is back?"

"The one who was in the Navy. He lost part of one leg in some navy battle. Now he works in the office with his father." Sean turned to her. "Do you want me to come in?"

Sharon opened the passenger door. "Of course."

Sean stepped out of the Austin and pointed at a door set in one corner of the ground floor. "We go this way." Sean opened the front door for her. "It's the first door on your left."

Sharon saw *McGregor and Son* etched in the glass framed by the office's oak door. She opened the door and stepped inside. She looked around at the reception desk. On either side were neat rows of books. Behind the desk stood three massive filing cabinets. The room proclaimed confident efficiency. She turned to her brother. "Are we in the right office?"

A man entered the reception area from one of the adjoining offices. "Who were you looking for?"

Sharon turned to face a man who was about six inches taller and perhaps two years older than she was. His black hair was cut and combed. His suit was blue and his blue tie knotted with a double Windsor. She held out her hand. "I'm Sharon Lacey."

The man smiled. "Of course you are. Father told me to expect you. My name is Rupert McGregor, Walter's son." He turned to Sean. "And this is?" Rupert offered his hand to Sean.

"My brother, Sean." Sharon watched with interest as the two shook hands.

Rupert looked over his shoulder at an open door. "Father?"

There was the sound of a chair being pushed back, papers hitting the floor, and footsteps on wood. While his son was neatly groomed and trimmed, Walter McGregor wore a rumpled brown tweed suit. "Ah, it is you." He smiled at Sharon and then turned to Sean. The lawyer's eyebrows were as thick as a hedge. The hair protruding from his ears and nostrils was at least as overgrown. "Good, you've brought Sean." Walter extended his hand and shook theirs in turn. He spun and gestured for them to enter his office. "Do you mind if Rupert joins us?"

"Not at all. I have very little time; I'm expected back this afternoon." Sharon stepped into the office. A glance told her that Rupert had not yet been able to apply his organizational skills to Walter's inner sanctum.

Walter shut the door behind them and cleared files piled on three chairs. "Please have a seat."

Sharon watched as Rupert stood in front of his chair, grabbed the oak arms, and kicked his left leg out. With a creaking of leather and metal, he sat down and crossed his right leg over his left.

"I've asked Rupert to join us because he's become my partner in the practice, and we work closely together," Walter said.

"It's okay with me." Sharon looked at Sean.

He shrugged as if to ask, "Why are you asking me?"

"You are aware that your grandmother is ill?" Walter asked.

"Yes, she seems to be reverting to her childhood," Sharon said.

"Three months ago, she came in to see me. She explained that she wasn't feeling like herself. She had me draw up documents to make me the executor of her will and expressed a desire that I should have power of attorney over her affairs. In her words, she wanted me to ensure that both her son and her granddaughter were looked after. She was very clear that she wanted each of you to have a half share of her estate." Walter leaned back in his chair. "I wanted to inform you of this new development. I expected to see you sooner, but the build-up leading to the invasion of France would explain why you haven't been free to travel here."

Sharon looked out of the window. In the distance, scarlet-jacketed riders trotted along the street. "Does my uncle know about this?" There was the call of a hunting horn, and Sharon blinked at a flash of insight. *The old guard senses the war is nearly over, and they've come to town to reassert themselves.*

Walter shook his head. "Your grandmother made it very clear that she wanted me to tell you of this new development and that she would tell Marmaduke."

Sharon turned and faced Walter. "Does he know?"

"I don't think so," Walter said.

"If I might interject here?" Rupert asked.

"Go ahead," Sharon said.

"If I understand the situation, you are not afraid for your personal welfare?" Rupert asked.

Sharon glanced at her brother and said, "No."

"Then this is a temporary situation," Rupert said.

"I don't understand," Sharon said.

"By all accounts, it would seem that the war will be over soon — within the year, perhaps. Then you and your brother will be free to live elsewhere. In point of fact, your entire family could move back to Canada. Or. . ." Rupert hesitated.

"Or?" Sharon asked.

"You could even afford to move to Australia, or wherever else in the world you would like to live. So that is why this is just a temporary situation." Rupert held his hands with palms up to emphasize his point.

"Oh." Sharon looked at Sean. "What do you think about moving away after the war?"

"Sounds grand, actually. The only complication is how Michael, Linda, and Honeysuckle will react." Sean raised his eyebrows and looked out of the window as another rider in a red coat clopped down the road.

"Where did that Jeep come from?" Sean parked the Austin on the gravel next to the stone two-storey Townsend house. They could see Linda, Honeysuckle, and a black-haired man wearing the blue of an RAF dress uniform. He was sitting and drinking what appeared to be coffee in the back garden where Honeysuckle's flowers bloomed.

Sharon waited for Sean to shut off the engine and apply the emergency brake. She smiled at him. "What say we go and meet this guy?"

"Who is he?" Sean opened his door.

Sharon watched the stranger turn toward them. She turned to Sean. "He's that pilot from yesterday — the one who's interested in Linda. His name is Milton. I wonder how he tracked us down?" She climbed out of the passenger side of the Austin, closed the door behind her, and walked toward the garden.

Milton stood up.

Sharon noted that Linda was evaluating him with frank interest.

Honeysuckle said, "I've just met Milton. He managed to find his way here. You didn't tell me that you told him where we lived."

Sharon looked at Linda, who sipped her coffee while she continued to study Milton. Sharon said, "We told the Wing Commander where we were going, and Milton must have been eavesdropping."

Milton smiled and turned to face Honeysuckle and Linda. "Guilty as charged."

Sean sat down across from Milton. He lifted one of Honeysuckle's thick ham sandwiches and began to eat.

Sharon sat down next to her brother, poured herself a cup of coffee, reached for a sandwich, and took a bite.

"You're from Calgary?" Milton asked Sharon.

She nodded.

"I'm from north and east of Edmonton; a place called Smoky Lake."

Sharon glanced at Linda and saw how she was staring at Milton.

"I come from the bush," Milton said.

"What exactly is the bush?" Linda asked.

Our lives just got very complicated. Sharon found she was a little jealous and excited at the prospect of Linda having someone in her life.

CHAPTER 7
[THURSDAY, JUNE 29, 1944]

Sharon looked outside of the cockpit of her Spitfire and saw that the wingtips had disappeared in the grey-white fog.

Rain gathered and skittered back along the outside of the canopy. More determined moisture made its way inside, gathered on the top of the Perspex canopy and dripped onto her slacks. The fabric on her knees was soaked through. She checked her instruments to ensure that she was on course, at altitude, and right side up.

"Shit!" Sharon exclaimed as she peered through the rain and fog in search of Longues. *My first trip into France in four years, and I can't see a bloody thing!*

The Spitfire flew into an open patch of sky. Sharon looked down and saw the Channel. She spotted cargo-laden landing craft making for the shoreline. The wake behind them told her she was headed in the right direction and — just a minute later! — she spotted the French coastline. She flew over four concrete domes, which she identified as Nazi gun positions apparently overtaken by Allied troops on the first day of the invasion. A few minutes after that, she was lined up to land at Longues. A green Very light flared up and disappeared into the grey belly of the overcast. Sharon landed and taxied over to what she hoped was the maintenance area.

Mechanics appeared at her wings and helped her guide the brand new Spitfire outside a hangar so that it would be ready for combat. She switched off, released her harness, and climbed out of the cockpit. "Any of you fellows know where the canteen is?"

"Over that way." One of the mechanics pointed in the general direction of a gathering of tents.

Sharon hefted her parachute over the shoulder of her sheepskin jacket and followed her nose to the camouflaged green of the largest tent. She dropped her parachute on the end of a table and made her way around to the urn, where she grabbed a cup of tea and was handed a sandwich wrapped in wax paper.

She sat down at her table, sipped the scalding tea, opened the wax paper, took a bite of the sandwich, and frowned at the greasy taste of Spam. She set it down on the table and reached for her cup. *On a day like today, even tea tastes good.* The warmth began to reach her fingers and toes. She took off her flying helmet, lifted her ponytail so that it hung over her collar, and wrapped her fingers around the metal cup.

One of the other pilots noticed her ponytail and elbowed a second in the ribs. The second RAF officer turned to look at her.

Someone looked outside of the tent. "Christ! It's Jerry!"

Sharon stood up, spilled her tea, and ran out of the tent. She saw a mechanic dive into a slit trench about fifty yards ahead. Two pilots from inside the tent passed her as they sprinted for cover. One of them slipped, slid, recovered, and jumped into the trench.

She looked over her right shoulder. A pair of long-nosed Focke-Wulf Ta 152s flew at treetop level. They were close enough for her to see the pilots hunched forward over their controls. She noted the fighters' light grey bellies, the green stretching from the top of the nose to behind the cockpit, the yellow stripes circling the back fuselage, and the black crosses. They opened fire with their cannons just as she dove into the trench and landed face-first in the muddy water.

A hand grabbed the collar of her Irvine jacket to lift her out of the muck. Another hand offered a handkerchief.

"Bonjour, Madame," one of the men said.

She saw that she was next to two pilots crouched in the trench and dressed in the dark blue of the Armée de l'Air.

One held out his hand. "Pierre." Then he pointed at the other pilot. "And this is Jacques."

Jacques said, "As usual, the Hun has spoiled the party. This is our first time on French soil in four years."

Sharon peered over the edge of the trench. Her eyes were drawn to an explosion. The Spitfire she'd delivered collapsed in a column of flame. She began to stand up.

Pierre grabbed her by the sleeve. "Wait another moment."

There was the incredible noise of anti-aircraft fire. Another pair of Focke-Wulfs appeared above the trees at the far end of the field. Their cannons winked. One of the fighters was hit by ground fire. It disintegrated in a flash of light and a cloud of debris. Sharon watched as the debris spilled onto the runway. Her mind filled with the image of one of the Nazi bombers she'd shot down. It was the recurring nightmare of a bomber hitting the ground and disappearing into a cloud of light, dust, and black smoke.

"Well, what was it like?" Ernie asked as Sharon tossed her parachute out the side door of the Anson. She stepped out on the wing root and sniffed at her mud-encrusted clothing. She looked down at her parachute and then at Ernie, who stood waiting for an answer.

Edgar stood next to Ernie. Both were on the concrete apron outside of the hangar door at White Waltham. The setting sun intensified the colours. The American was at least as interested as his Canadian companion in what Sharon had to tell them. "Well?"

"Minutes after I landed, the airfield was strafed and the Spit I delivered was burning. It was a complete waste of time." She stepped down onto the concrete.

"Not really," Ernie said.

"How's that?" Sharon asked.

"You're back safe," Edgar said.

"But your clothes are a little worse for wear." Ernie smiled.

She looked down at the dried mud on her jacket and her slacks.

"A couple of French pilots helped me up out of the mud."

"How is the invasion going?" Ernie asked.

"Hard to tell. I could hardly see my wingtips for most of the way over there. After I landed, most of the time was spent in a slit trench. FW 190s kept strafing the airfield. All I can tell you is that the invasion is moving inland and the Nazis are counterattacking." *I need to get cleaned up.* "Anything new?"

Ernie and Edgar looked at one another.

"Hurry up. Tell me. I need a change of clothes." *What's happened now?*

"A new pilot arrived," Edgar said.

"Good, we're short of pilots." Sharon unzipped her Irvine jacket. *I hope the mud washes off easily.* She scraped at a clot of dried mud with her thumbnail.

Ernie was uncharacteristically quiet.

"She was looking for you," Edgar said.

"What's her name?" Sharon peeled off her jacket and checked the wool on the inside.

"Lady Ginette." Edgar looked at Ernie.

Sharon faced Ernie. "You're being very quiet. What's going on?"

Ernie stuck out his chin and growled. "The last time I opened my mouth to say what I thought, I ended up here. I like it here."

"There you are!" The voice was female, piercing and plummy.

Sharon turned and saw the approach of a round-faced woman. She was Sharon's height, and wore bobbed black hair and a toothy smile. "I've heard so much about Sharon Lacey. I'm Lady Ginette Elam!"

Sharon caught a whiff of perfume. The woman smelled of lilac. Sharon was immediately reminded of her mother.

Ginette said, "Excuse us," to Ernie and Edgar, then put her arm around Sharon's shoulder and guided her toward the dispersal hut.

In a matter of ten minutes, all of the pilots inside were gathered around Ginette and Sharon. "You must know that Miss Lacey is an ace!"

Sharon blushed at being the centre of attention — especially at finding herself part of the conversation and not merely the surreptitious object of it.

CHAPTER 8

[SATURDAY, AUGUST 19, 1944]

"It was clear sailing. The airfield was dusty." Sharon swiped at her slacks. There was a puff of dust. She looked up at the two men who were waiting for firsthand news of what was up on the continent.

Ernie and Edgar recognized her thousand-yard stare, looked at each other, then turned and frowned at her.

"You want the truth?" Sharon asked.

They nodded.

"I blundered over Falais." *You know that big Allied victory we've been hearing about? We've finally broken out of Normandy.*

"And?" Ernie asked.

"I was flying at about eight hundred feet in a brand new Spitfire. Below me, the roadway was clogged with burned-out trucks, tanks, and bodies — miles of bodies. The stink of rotting corpses was so strong, it was almost like flying into a wall. I couldn't wait to get out of there and land at the airfield. Even after I got there, the stink was still in the air. Someone told me they thought there were ten thousand German dead."

"Serves the bastards right, after the way the ss executed Canadian prisoners at Ardenne Abbey," Ernie said.

Sharon looked at him and shook her head. *Somehow it doesn't add up. You didn't smell the rot. You didn't see what I saw.* "I need a shower."

She walked to the dispersal hut.

As was usual now, Lady Ginette was holding court with whichever pilots were stopping for a meal or a cuppa.

"After I was finished flight training, they called the school Lady Ginette's Flying Circus in honour of me!"

There was the obligatory roar of laughter from the pilots sitting and standing around the lady's table.

Sharon walked the other way to Mother's booth, where he was talking on the phone. She unzipped, set her parachute down on a nearby chair, then dropped her helmet and goggles on top of it. *I must look a mess.*

Mother looked up and wrinkled his nose. "Where have you been?"

"Falais." Sharon knew she need say no more to Mother.

"War's a filthy business. There's another priority delivery for you." Mother handed her a chit. "See if her majesty there can get up off of her throne and do her job."

Mother's tone stopped Sharon short. "Has something happened?"

He looked up at her and thought for a moment. "How did you get your present job?"

Where is this coming from and where is it going? "d'Erlanger asked me to do it."

Mother pointed his index finger at her nose. "You earned it. You proved yourself as a pilot and a leader. This place is running along and doing its job because you know what you're doing and you're not afraid to roll up your sleeves and get done what needs doing. Not everyone in this country earns her way like that."

"Mother. I'm tired and need a shower. What are you trying to tell me?" She glanced at the chit and her eyebrows rose.

"There are some who kept their fingernails clean and lived away from London on their estates; some even had fascist leanings. Those ones waited until now, when the war is nearly won, to join up so they'd have stories to tell at dinner parties when the fighting's over." Again, he pointed his finger at Sharon. "Then there are the others who've done the dirty work. Now that the job is nearly done, people like you need to watch out because you haven't been bred to live in the world of posh politics. Just because you don't want the glory and have earned your way doesn't mean that everyone else is like that."

Just when I thought this was getting easier. Sharon felt weariness settle onto her shoulders. "Shit."

"A very apt word to describe what's been going on since her ladyship arrived. Now go get cleaned up and I'll have her majesty ready her chariot." Mother picked up the phone and waved Sharon away.

After a quick shower and change of clothes, she grabbed her parachute and walked out to the Anson. She eased inside the Anson's side door.

Lady Ginette sat in the pilot's seat. "Welcome aboard!" She started the first engine.

Sharon settled herself in. *Mother has only said something about a pilot on three occasions. One was a drunk who was endangering lives. The second was an accident waiting to happen, and the third is sitting in the cockpit of the Anson.*

Sharon watched as Ginette worked the controls and was impressed with the woman's abilities as a pilot. Her hands were soft and confident, she kept her head out of the office, and she was always one step ahead. *A pilot always needs to be one step ahead.*

After landing, Sharon said, "Thanks for the ride!"

Ginette smiled and waved.

"How long have you been flying?" Sharon opened the door.

Ginette held up ten fingers and nodded in the direction of the aircraft parked on the apron. "Hope you don't find out why they call it a meat box!"

Sharon stepped out into the prop wash. She took about ten steps, turned, and watched the Anson taxi away. *I'll have to do some checking on this one. That was a rather nasty thing to say to any pilot.*

She turned around and spotted her delivery. The twin-engined fighter balanced on tricycle landing gear. Its canopy glinted in the sunlight.

"This'll put those 616 boys at Manston in their place." A mechanic stepped out of the hangar and onto the concrete apron where the Meteor sat in its camouflage grey and green. The mechanic was dressed in immaculate white coveralls; his black hair was slicked back with pomade.

Sharon looked at him. "Will you show me the taps, please?"

The mechanic nodded and became suddenly businesslike. "No offense. It's just that those boys at 616 think they're a pretty elite bunch because they're the first squadron to be equipped with a jet."

Sharon smiled, set her parachute on the wing root, and did her walk around. *Don't tell him he looks like a movie star playing a mechanic. He'll get all puffed up.* She pulled her hair back, tied it into a ponytail, and tucked it under her leather helmet. Then she strapped the parachute on.

The mechanic climbed onto the wing, then waited for her to follow and get settled in the cockpit. He watched as she tested the controls. "The ailerons get heavy at high speed just like the Spitfire and the Tempest," he said. "The various controls are in the usual places. The only thing that takes a bit of adjusting to is the throttle."

Sharon nodded, smiled, and slid the canopy closed. The mechanic got off the wing and waited by the start-up cart. Sharon started first one engine and then the other. She watched the mechanic slide the cart away. He gave her a wave.

Sharon enjoyed the forward view without an engine and a propeller in the way. She slid the throttle forward. The Meteor inched ahead and gathered itself.

After takeoff, she was surprised by the quiet, since all of the engine noise was behind her. She flew for the south of London at three hundred and eighty miles per hour during the half-hour flight. *There's nothing to do but concentrate on flying, familiarize yourself with the Meteor's handling, and find the airfield.* Her mind was cleared of all of the other duties awaiting her on the ground.

The landing was smooth, and she taxied over to a hangar where two other camouflaged jets were parked outside.

After handing over the aircraft, she made her way to the mess, where she caught the scent of frying bacon. Inside, she sat down at a table with a cup of coffee and a plate of bacon and scrambled eggs. She expected to be left alone to eat and was not disappointed.

One egg later, a man sat down beside her. *Just eat your meal, drink your coffee, and look straight ahead.*

"How was your first trip in the Meteor?" Michael asked.

She turned, caught the smile on her husband's face, and threw her arms around his neck. He pulled her in close and she savoured the scent of him.

"What are you doing here?" Sharon asked.

"I know the squadron leader and was asked to come here to have a chat. So, you know, a call here and there, and here we are." Michael looked at her half-eaten meal. "I'm famished. Mind if I join you? These RAF types still get the best food."

A few minutes later, he sat down next to her and tucked into bacon and eggs. "Next best thing to being at home in my mother's kitchen."

Sharon nodded as she folded a piece of bacon in a slice of toast.

"I hear you're considering moving back to Canada after the war." Michael tried to make the comment seem offhand, but he failed.

"It was a suggestion by Rupert McGregor. He thinks that it's an option worth considering. He brought it up when I met with him the end of June." Sharon put her elbows on the table.

"Apparently, Sean thinks it's a fait accompli. My mother wrote me a letter. She's in a panic and assumes we're leaving within the month."

Sharon took a deep breath and looked around at the pilots there. Soon after the invasion, there was hope that the war would be over by Christmas. The reality was settling in. "Look, I should have mentioned it to you, but I haven't seen you in over a month. Yes, I've thought about it, especially lately. I'm so tired of the war. And this morning. . ."

"This morning?" Michael put his knife and fork on the plate.

"I flew over the Falais Gap. The smell was, well, it was. . ."

"Indescribable?"

Sharon nodded and felt tears in her eyes. *Don't you dare cry!*

"And it will probably get worse before it gets better," Michael added, looking at the pieces of bacon left on his plate — treats he'd saved for the end of the meal.

"What's that supposed to mean?" She leaned in closer.

He dropped his voice. "More reports have been coming in.

Something the Nazis call the Final Solution."

"What's that?"

"Elimination of Jews in all occupied territories." Michael leaned his chin on his fists.

"Mass deportations?" Sharon asked.

"Extermination."

The word hung over the table. It reminded Sharon of the stink of death rising over Falais that morning.

An hour into the car ride to White Waltham, Sharon broke the silence. "I'm sorry, I should have let you know what the lawyer said to us."

"We're almost at Chertsey. Like to stop for tea?" Michael smiled as he added, "It's been impossible for both of us. The bloody war is always getting in the way. I just keep hoping that we're near the end and then can lead some kind of normal life afterward."

"That would be nice. It seems like it's still a long way away. Think they'll have some coffee?"

They stopped at one end of a stone bridge that stepped its arches over the River Thames. In the late-day sunshine, the grass was greener, the river sparkled, and the stonework on the bridge was etched with shadow.

"What's that?" Sharon pointed at the statue of a woman holding the clapper of a bell.

"Blanche Heriot." Michael pulled over and stopped alongside the statue. The engine ticked over. "She saved her lover during the War of the Roses."

"War." Sharon looked at the statue. *War is part of the culture here.*

"Where would we live if we moved to Canada?" Michael looked at the river and the bridge that spanned it.

"I have a house. It's on the edge of the city. Near the Elbow River. Quite nice, actually." She turned to see what he was looking at. "Not very far from downtown."

"Big enough for the three of us?" he asked.

Sharon nodded. "Yes." *What's got me thinking about the future? For so long, there was no thought of tomorrow, only today.*

"A week after the invasion, I started to think beyond the war. That there might be a future for us after the war. I was afraid." Michael turned to look at her.

"Afraid of what?"

"When I figure that out for myself, I'll let you know."

"What do you know about Lady Ginette Elam?"

Michael smiled. "You prefer to talk shop?"

Sharon shrugged. "Mother said something funny to me about people staying out of the war until now. He implied that she needed stories to tell at parties after the war is over."

"Mother has a sharp mind." Michael stared at the statue. "There's a fascist connection in the Elam family. Before the war, they supported Mussolini. You know, the advantages of having the trains run on time and all of that. When it looked like Hitler and Mussolini might win the war, some opportunists backed the winner. Now that it looks like we'll win the war, they're backing us."

"You make it sound very cold-blooded." She heard the bleakness in her voice.

"Self-preservation is a pretty powerful motivator."

"So you're saying I should watch my back?" Sharon looked at her husband and saw the weariness in his eyes.

"I'm afraid that Mother and I agree on this one. Lady Ginette's first priority is Lady Ginette. And she will see you as a minor obstacle if you happen to get in her way."

CHAPTER 9

"Would you write me a letter?" Edgar was up to his elbows in one of the Anson's engines.

Sharon found herself studying Edgar as he looked at her while his right hand tightened a nut with a socket wrench. She asked, "What kind of letter?"

"A reference letter for the 332nd in Italy. If you and Ernie write me reference letters, I'll have a shot with the Red Tails." Edgar grunted as he snugged up a nut and moved to the next.

"Can I write it up when I get back?" She hefted her parachute as she heard the duty Anson starting up. "There's a big push on, and I need to deliver a Dakota."

Edgar nodded.

Two hours later, she was on approach on the east coast of England. Ahead of her, a Dakota took off trailing a glider. Beyond, a stream of transport aircraft headed east over the Channel.

Her Dakota's twin engines ticked over. Its long wings transferred every bump in air boiling from the wake of so many other aircraft. The turbulence forced her to constantly work the control wheel and rudder pedals. By the time she was on the taxiway, she was exhausted from the effort.

The tower ordered her toward a group of men gathered next to a petrol bowser. She worked throttle, rudder, and brakes to get the Dakota onto the refueling apron.

After shutting down, she looked out the left side as a man with rolled-up sleeves hauled a hose onto the wing and began to top up the tanks.

Sharon gathered her operating manual and logbook, stuffed them into a green over-the-shoulder canvas bag, and walked downhill to the rear door.

It opened before she could get there. A helmeted head poked in, spotted her, and said, "Hang on, boys."

She made her way to the open side door. A soldier looked up at her. He was wearing a helmet, his face was greased with green camouflage paint, and he was loaded down with parachutes, a Sten gun, and enough ammunition to start his own tiny war. *He can't be a year older than Sean.*

The commando held out his hand and helped her out of the plane. Too polite to refuse, she took his hand.

The waiting commandos parted to let her pass. They smelled of sweat, greasepaint, cigarettes, and gun oil. When she stepped past the last of the men, one of them said, "All right, boys. Off we go!"

One of the commandos said, "Off on another of Monty's fuckin' escapades."

She turned to watch the men climb aboard the Dakota in its camouflage green with the white and black invasion stripes on the undersides of the wings. *I wonder how many of them will be alive at the end of today?*

A half-hour later, she sat in the last seat of the duty Anson as it flew back to White Waltham. Out the window, she could see the stream of aircraft — all manner of two- and four-engined aircraft — flying east.

After another delivery, she returned to White Waltham.

Ernie and Edgar waited outside of the hangar as she walked away from the air taxi. Sharon checked her watch and saw that it was nearly six o'clock. She turned at the sound of a Jeep approaching at high speed.

Beck skidded to a stop, pointed at Edgar, then hitched his thumb to indicate that Edgar should get in the back. Edgar climbed in, the MP executed a U-turn and roared off.

"We'd better get busy on those letters," Sharon said.

It took about an hour between bites of beans and potatoes to write out the details of both letters. They left the mutton untouched.

"Mother said he'll get them typed up for us." Sharon took the two handwritten letters and set them to one side.

"What do we do if Edgar leaves? Things are running smoothly right now." Ernie looked at the mutton on his plate. He used the back of his left hand to push the plate to his left, then crossed his arms.

"I'll have to find a replacement for him."

"I can't blame him for leaving. He's been telling me about the way he gets treated." Ernie looked at the other side of the room.

"On the American base?" Sharon followed Ernie's gaze and saw a clutch of pilots gathered around a table with Lady Ginette at its head.

"There, here, back home." Ernie turned his eyes to Sharon. "Makes you wonder if some of the Nazis are on our side."

"What's going on here?" Sharon made eye contact with Ernie as she felt the anger boiling in her belly.

"You gotta know your place in the pecking order around here, if you know what I mean." Ernie cocked his head in the direction of the good Lady and her entourage.

"Hello."

Ernie and Sharon turned to face a young woman. She was taller than Ernie, had prominent front teeth, freckles, and unruly curly red hair, and wore a uniform that was a size too big. "Molly Hume," the woman said, extending her right hand. "I'm a new replacement pilot fresh out of Haddenham."

Sharon took the hand and was surprised by the strength in the wiry grip of the long fingers. "Sharon Lacey."

"Ernie." He stood and shook Molly's hand.

"Have a seat. What part of Scotland are you from?" Sharon asked.

Molly smiled. "Glasgow. It's that obvious?"

Sharon smiled back. "Where are you billeted?"

"Mother's taking care of all that. How come everyone calls him Mother?" Molly sat down next to Sharon and across from Ernie.

"Baa haaa haaa!" The comment was followed by impolitely suppressed laughter from Lady Ginette's table.

Sharon stood up, turned, and looked at the men and women at Ginette's table. None met her gaze. One muttered, "Sorry."

Sharon sat back down, felt the heat of rage on her face, and looked at Molly. "Sorry about that."

"Assholes," Ernie said.

"When do I start flying?" Molly's cheeks were red from embarrassment.

"Tomorrow morning. I'll see you here at six," Sharon said.

That evening, she opened the door to the cottage and found Linda inside, sitting in the massive wing-backed chair with the floral print. "Come on," Linda said. "We're going out for supper. My treat."

They drove Michael and Sharon's MG two-seat sports car with the wire wheels. It carried them to the Shire Horse pub at Littlewick Green.

Sharon parked outside of the white picket fence in front of the brick pub with its white-framed windows.

"It's a beautiful evening. Okay if we sit outside?" Sharon read the chalkboard menu out front of the pub. "They've got fresh fish. A real treat!"

They climbed out of the MG, closed the doors, walked through the gate, and sat at one of the tables outside the pub's front door.

After ordering a pint each and fresh fish suppers, Sharon sat back. "So what's up?"

"You don't think I can take you out for supper with no strings attached?" Linda tried to sound offended as she pushed a wayward strand of red hair away from her ear.

Sharon went to reply, decided to wait, and reached for her pint. It was amber, room temperature, and gentle on the tongue.

Linda looked past Sharon at the flowers along a two-foot-tall hedge.

Just wait, she'll get to it, Sharon thought.

Linda took a sip from her pint. "Lovely evening, isn't it?"

Sharon shook her head and put down her glass. "I give up."

"Well then, if you must. Honeysuckle is still upset that you're contemplating moving back to Canada." Linda crossed her left leg over her right.

"As I explained to Michael, Rupert McGregor brought it up when we met with him. Sean loves the idea, and I haven't had the time to give it much thought, to tell you the truth." Sharon studied Linda's reaction and saw that her sister-in-law was chewing the inside of her cheek.

"Honeysuckle thinks that if you decide to emigrate, she'll never see any of you again." Linda put her hands on the table. Her long fingers reached for the glass.

"Maybe she'd like to come along?" Sharon said, before considering the consequences.

"So you *are* thinking about it!" Linda pointed a finger at her friend and sister-in-law.

"Look. I came over here to find my father, saw him killed, became a killer, and found out I had a brother. At my first meeting with my mother's brother, he tried to rape me. Now he's doing his best to destroy my reputation. On most days, I might as well be a ghost at White Waltham after the rumours he's spread about me." Sharon closed her mouth, surprised at the rage she felt.

"You also met me, your brother Sean, married Michael, and became part of my family." Again, Linda pointed her finger at Sharon.

I wish you would stop pointing that finger at me. Sharon took a deep breath. "Thank you for bringing my dilemma into such sharp focus."

"Besides, that's not the only reason I took you out for supper." Linda looked sideways at Sharon.

"Ladies." They both looked up as the waiter, an ancient man with perfect posture, set two plates of fish and fresh baby potatoes with dill in front of them.

Sharon stared at the bounty before her. She looked at Linda, who smiled. "With food like this, maybe we *are* winning the war." She picked up her fork and waited for her friend.

Sharon speared a potato and popped it into her mouth. Then she opened her mouth and breathed in cool air. "Hot!" She doused the hot potato with a mouth full of beer.

"I need a favour, and I don't want any questions." Linda pointed her fork at her friend. Sharon began to inhale cooler air as she chewed the potato. "I need a forty-eight hour pass for the twenty-first and twenty-second of this month." Linda cut a piece of fish with her fork, then speared the morsel, and touched it to her tongue. She blew on it.

Sharon chewed. *It must be a man.* "Milton."

"I said no questions." Linda popped the piece of fish into her mouth.

"What's his last name? Now, that was a question." Sharon cut a potato in half, speared one side, and blew on it.

Linda rolled her eyes. "If you must know, it's Cardinal."

"So you *have* been talking." Sharon put the tip of her tongue on the potato. "These are so good."

Linda put her knife and fork down. "Well?"

"When was the last time you had a leave? By that I mean, all you do is fly, and then you fly some more. The last time you had a day off was when we flew the Storch home."

Linda blushed.

"I'll talk with Mother in the morning. Just write the dates down for me so I get them right." Sharon began to dig into her supper.

"I hope you won't tell Michael or my mother about this."

Sharon shook her head. "Mum's the word."

CHAPTER 10
[TUESDAY, SEPTEMBER 19, 1944]

Mother said, "There's fog in the forecast. If the weather begins to close in, just put it down at the nearest airfield and wait for it to clear. The war will go on just fine without you." Sharon watched as Mother handed Molly a chit.

"Where are you off to?" Sharon asked.

"It says a Magister at RAF Upavon." Molly revealed all of her healthy teeth as she smiled.

"Neigh!"

Sharon turned in time to see a pilot using her right foot like a hoof. The woman, whose name was Patricia, turned to Lady Ginette for approval. "Patricia? Something wrong with your foot?" Sharon asked.

Patricia was shorter than Lady Ginette and about fifty pounds lighter. The rouge was bright on her cheeks. Still, her face reddened.

Lady Ginette did not turn around.

Sharon turned back to Molly. "Remember what Mother said about the weather." Molly nodded, then hefted her parachute and shoulder bag before making her way to the duty Anson.

Mother handed a chit to Sharon. She took it.

He used his index finger to indicate Sharon should come closer. In a whisper, he said, "I've got the last Swordfish delivery for Scapa

Flow." He held up a chit. "This'll keep Patricia out of trouble for a day or two." He smiled.

Sharon said, "Thank you," and left.

Three hours later, cloud and fog closed in, forcing her away from her destination. Sharon checked the maps in her side pockets. She turned the fighter west in an ever-narrowing sky. Ten minutes later, she spotted Kirkbride just inland from Moricambe Bay on her left. The airfield was on the northwest coast of England, closer to Belfast than to London. The runway was an X at the centre of yellow fields of rape. Sharon throttled back, and as the speed of the Corsair dropped, she lowered the flaps, then the landing gear. She looked west, where the fog was sifting in from the bay just as it disappeared from view. Her hands worked the controls instinctively. *Just sixty more seconds and I'll be on the ground.* She took a long, slow breath to calm her nerves and clear her mind. This kind of weather could kill a pilot as surely as the guns of an enemy fighter. She lined up on finals, eased the throttle back, and checked that her wheels were down.

The runway disappeared ahead of the blue nose of the navy fighter. She looked out the right side of the canopy as the wheels touched down. When she reached the end of the runway, she checked the location of the tower and turned right to taxi toward the green hangars next to it.

The fog wafted over her canopy and the tower disappeared. She concentrated on staying lined up on the taxiway by looking out the left side at the edge of the tarmac. The fog thickened and she could no longer see the edge.

Using her mental map of the airfield, she turned the fighter to the left, bumped onto the grass, swung the tail around with a burst of throttle, and shut down. More than thirteen feet of propeller rolled to a halt. She checked to make sure all of the switches were off before she slid back the canopy, stepped out onto the fighter's gull wing, and jumped down off the trailing edge onto the ground.

She stood still and listened.

A whistle blew. The shrinking metal of the cooling engine ticked as she ducked under the belly of the Corsair and followed the sound.

The whistle blew twenty more times before she felt the concrete apron under her heels.

"I can hear ye, lassie." The thick Scottish accent was like music. Sharon walked toward the voice, stepped inside the open door, and stood face to face with a sandy-haired man who was almost as tall as she was. He wore RAF blue and a smile. "A lucky Canadian, I see." He pointed at the shoulder flashes on her battle jacket.

"Could I please use the phone?" she asked.

"Right over there." The Scotsman pointed ahead and to her right.

"I was supposed to make it to Glasgow this morning. I need to let them know where I ended up." Sharon eased past him, intent on her call to Mother. *I hope all of the other pilots are safe.*

The fog stayed the rest of the day. Sharon slept in her uniform on a cot that was reserved for occasions like these.

CHAPTER 11
[WEDNESDAY, SEPTEMBER 20, 1944]

The engines of the duty Anson shut down. Sharon was first out the door. She carried her kit to dispersal, located in the red one-storey building at White Waltham. Mother greeted her at the door. The look on his face told her that her fears were well-founded.

"How many missing?" she asked.

"One."

"Who?" Sharon set her kit down inside on a table.

"Molly took delivery of the Magister, but didn't reach Upavon." Mother waited for Sharon's reaction.

She looked out the doorway. "Is the Storch available?"

Mother nodded. "I think so. Let me check." He went out the door and around to the hangar.

Sharon searched out a cup of coffee in the empty canteen as she planned a route in her mind, drawing a mental line from the pickup point to Upavon.

Mother tapped her on the shoulder. Ernie and Edgar were pushing the Storch out of the hangar when she arrived at the open door.

"I need another pair of eyes in the back seat." Sharon put her parachute inside and helped push the single-engined aircraft out onto the grass.

She did a slow, deliberate walk around to check the aircraft. *Keep your mind clear!*

Ernie stepped into a fresh pair of coveralls. "Edgar says he'll hold down the fort."

In five minutes, they were airborne and headed south and west.

Ernie kept a lookout on one side while Sharon covered the other. They flew at eight hundred feet above ground.

Forty minutes later, after flying over every shade of green imaginable, Ernie tapped Sharon on the shoulder.

They found out later that the crash was on the northern face of a place called Milton Hill. The tail of the open-cockpit two-seater trainer was recognizable. The rest of the aircraft was a tangled mass of wreckage.

Sharon eased back on the throttle and slowed the aircraft to make a low, slow pass over the crash site. The yellow underside of one wing was about fifty feet downhill from most of the rest of the wreck. Molly's twisted body was visible in what was left of the cockpit.

Sharon turned for another pass, glanced over her shoulder, and saw Ernie shake his head. They flew over the wreckage three times, hoping for any sign that Molly was alive, but there was no movement. Sharon dropped the flaps, adjusted the throttle, and swung around to land up the hill.

She was on finals when she felt Ernie's hand on her shoulder. "It won't make a fucking bit of difference."

Sharon felt her shoulders drop as she opened the throttle and eased over the top of the hill, flying on to Upavon. *Keep your mind on the job,* she thought as she lined up on finals and landed.

It took more than four hours for the rescue crew to find the wreck, recover the body, and return to Upavon. Sharon stayed to identify the body, then flew back with Ernie to White Waltham.

Edgar was waiting. He saw the grim exhaustion in Sharon's face and helped her from the Storch without saying a word. He put his arm around her shoulder and held her close. He smelled of motor oil, soap, and coffee.

"I guess I'd better let everyone know." Sharon turned to get her kit.

"We'll take care of your gear," Edgar said.

She walked around the corner of the hangar toward the dispersal hut. Through the white-framed windows, she could see the faces of pilots turned her way.

Mother greeted her at the door. There was a strange look on his face. One side of his mouth was turned down. He put his hand on her shoulder, but said nothing. *He's already heard, but is waiting for me to make the announcement.* Sharon looked at the coffee urn, thought better of grabbing a cup, then turned to the pilots sitting at tables. Expectant faces quietly studied her.

"Molly Hume flew into a hill in the fog. Her body was found in the wreckage." Sharon felt her shoulders sag.

A wail erupted. It was Lady Ginette. Three of the pilots crowded around the woman as the volume of her grief increased.

Sharon stood there open-mouthed. *But you and your clan treated Molly like dirt!*

"But she was so young! I can't believe it. I saw her just yesterday. It could happen to me!" Lady Ginette said.

Sharon shook her head, turned on her heel, and went out the door.

CHAPTER 12

[WEDNESDAY, SEPTEMBER 27, 1944]

"You've been awfully quiet," Linda said as she walked beside Sharon on the way back to the cottage.

The evening sun was low, and it caught them on the sides of their faces. The greenery was lit with oranges and yellows. Shadows ran long across the gravel lane.

Sharon shrugged.

"You haven't even asked about Milton and me." Linda lifted the bag off of her left shoulder and switched it to her right.

"So, how was your leave with Milton?" Sharon looked ahead along the lane where trees provided shade when the sun was high, thus keeping part of the lane cool even on the hottest of days.

"Fun." Linda tried to see what Sharon was looking at.

"Oh." Sharon looked at her friend and saw that Linda was smiling. "This is a switch."

"Oh?" Linda tucked her left hand inside Sharon's elbow.

Be careful how you say this, Sharon thought.

"Well?" Linda squeezed her friend's arm.

"I'm thinking."

"Out with it," Linda said.

"I'm the one who's melancholy, and you're the one who's looking on the bright side of things." Sharon turned to her friend, tried to smile, and succeeded, sort of.

"That wasn't so bad. Was I that awful to be around?" Linda continued to hold her sister-in-law close.

Sharon thought, *Don't answer that!*

"My mother says that when my father came back from the first war, he was a different person. When I was a child, he would often wake up screaming after a nightmare. There was one name in particular that he would scream. It was Robert. Mother told me that father saw Robert killed. They had been friends in school." Linda hesitated for a moment and looked past Sharon. Sharon went to say something, then stopped.

"It was such a horrible experience he tried to forget," Linda went on, "but the memories would wake him up in the night. I remember the look on my father's face the morning after a nightmare. He had a haunted look. A faraway gaze. It made him look like he was being hunted by something he could never escape from. That's the way I was after the crash and fire. I would see that faraway, haunted expression in the mirror after every nightmare. Now I see it in your eyes." Linda hugged Sharon around the shoulders.

Sharon pointed to the front of the cottage. A black Humber saloon car was parked at the door. To her, it resembled a hearse. She felt her pulse beginning to pound. *What's happened?*

A man stepped out of the back door. He had wild grey hair, wore a jacket and tie, and pants that appeared to be several sizes too large. He waved.

"Father?" Linda released Sharon and picked up the pace. She wrapped her arms around him. "How much weight have you lost?" He smelled of pipe smoke and Scotch.

"A stone or two." He smiled.

He looks even older when he smiles, Sharon thought.

He lifted his head, spotted Sharon, and waved her over. She hugged Harry and thought, *Christ, he's skin and bone!* "Come on in and we'll fix you something to eat."

Harry went to the back of the car, opened the boot, picked up a basket, closed the hatch, and tapped the window. The driver, who wore an olive green military uniform, started the engine and pulled away.

"Doesn't he want something to eat as well?" Sharon asked.

"I was hoping to have the two of you to myself for an hour." Harry followed them into the house and set the basket on the kitchen table before returning to the front room. He sat in the wing-backed chair. "Your aunt always had hideous taste."

"She still on the coast?" Sharon asked. In the kitchen, they could hear leather and wicker tattling as Linda lifted the lid of the basket.

"And being a tremendous burden to her children and grandchildren, as I understand it. Consider yourselves very fortunate, despite the decor." Harry leaned back in the chair and closed his eyes.

Linda stepped into the room. She had cans and jars clutched to her chest. "Where did you find all of this?"

Harry didn't open his eyes. "In the evenings, I often walk around London and look to see what I can find. Lately, there's been more to find in the shops near where I work."

"Do you want some help?" Sharon asked.

"Sit and talk with him. I'll only be a minute." Linda stepped back into the kitchen.

"How have you been?" Harry leaned forward.

"Okay," Sharon said.

"No, she's not. She's haunted by nightmares," Linda said. There was the clatter of a plate on the kitchen table.

Harry took a long look at his daughter-in-law. "There are those who will tell you to bury those memories. I tried that. It doesn't work. There is a friend of mine who I see from time to time. He was in the same regiment as me. When I need to, we get together and talk about it."

"I keep thinking about the boys I killed. Seeing Molly in the wreckage has brought all of those memories back with a vengeance." Sharon sat down on the settee upholstered in a garish pattern of yellow, pink, and red chrysanthemums.

"Molly?" Harry put his elbow on the arm of the chair.

"A young pilot. She crashed in bad weather earlier this month."

Linda brought in two plates, one with cheeses and jams, the other with biscuits.

"Have you ever killed anyone?" Sharon asked.

Harry nodded. "Both directly and indirectly. In the first war, I killed with a rifle and twice with a bayonet. Nowadays, young men die when I make a mistake in planning."

Linda placed a platter on the coffee table. It was a collage of rare treats. She picked up a slice of cheese biscuit, popped it into her mouth, and asked, "What's happened, Father?"

"Market Garden." His voice was just above a whisper.

"The papers say it was the biggest airborne operation in history." Linda offered the plate to Sharon, who took a biscuit and held it in her right hand. Linda got up and offered some to her father.

"No, thank you." He waved the food away.

"The news we're getting is that bridges were captured." Sharon leaned forward until her elbows were on her knees.

"Thousands of young men died. Monty and his cronies wouldn't listen to me. They wanted the war to be over by Christmas. We all want that. I tried to tell them that the German defenses were too strong. That we would need more armoured support. I couldn't make them listen." Harry's eyes looked at Linda, then at Sharon.

"You can't hold yourself responsible because others won't listen." Sharon stood up.

Linda said, "You were part of the invasion planning. That succeeded."

"Still, thousands of young men died." Harry looked at his watch. "The driver will be here in five minutes." He pointed at Sharon. "Please sit back down. I came to warn the pair of you."

Sharon sat down and gave Linda a worried look. Linda stared at her father.

Harry said, "I want the two of you to promise me you'll stay out of London over the winter."

"Why?" Linda asked.

"Just promise!" Harry slammed his hand on the arm of the chair.

"Would you please explain?" Sharon saw tears forming in Linda's eyes.

"The V-1 is only the first of Hitler's vengeance weapons. We're getting reports of another. I'm certain it will be aimed at London. I would like my children to survive the war. At this point, it's all I'm asking for." Harry stood up.

Linda stood.

Sharon asked, "What about Michael?"

"He's at Bletchley Park. I'm hoping he will be safe there until it's over." Harry turned for the door. "I have to get back."

Sharon looked at Linda, who appeared to be afraid to step forward or back. Sharon moved forward. "I'd like a hug before you go."

Harry turned and smiled. "Of course." Sharon held him close. He moved his lips close to her ear. "Lady Ginette is no match for you. You must be a descendant of Boudicca." He released her.

"Linda, get over here and give him a hug." Sharon took her friend by the elbow and pulled her closer until she put her arms around her father. They followed Harry outside, closed the door, and watched him until he drove away.

"Who the hell was Boudicca?" Sharon asked.

CHAPTER 13
[SATURDAY, OCTOBER 14, 1944]

After her fourth delivery of the day, Sharon almost fell out of the back door of the duty Anson.

She lifted her face to the sun as the other pilots walked past her. She opened her eyes and saw Ernie inside the hangar. He was drinking from a stainless steel thermos cup, sitting on half of an engine cowling and contemplating the guts of another Anson engine.

Sharon hefted her parachute onto her right shoulder and walked to the hangar. She inhaled a familiar mélange: grease, oil, gasoline, dope, and paint. The sound of her flying boots on the concrete made Ernie turn.

"Long day?" Sharon looked around the interior for Edgar.

"He's gone back to his base." Ernie had a grim look as he raised his thermos cup.

"What happened?" Sharon felt a dread she couldn't put into words.

"He got his transfer to the 332nd in Italy. Friday will be his last day." Ernie returned to staring at the engine.

"Shit," Sharon said.

"Exactly." Ernie sipped from his cup.

"Are you getting drunk?" Sharon asked.

"You bet."

"Where's the bottle?" she asked.

Ernie pointed to the office at the back of the hangar. "Bottom right-hand drawer."

"Mind if I join you?" Sharon walked toward the rear of the hangar.

"Be my guest."

CHAPTER 14

[WEDNESDAY, OCTOBER 18, 1944]

"Come on, Linda, we're going to be late." Sharon stood at the bottom of the stairs. She reached for her newest blue jacket, looked at the ATA tie and hat, shook her head, and checked herself in the mirror. *Michael and Milton will be there, too.* She felt the tingling thrill of anticipation that came with seeing her husband after more than a month.

Linda wore a white blouse, carefully pressed trousers, and fresh red lipstick as she came down the stairs. "What's got your wind up?"

"We're late." Sharon turned and opened the door. "You look very nice."

"As do you. You don't often wear your hair down. Michael will be impressed. I hope he and Milton will hit it off." Linda closed the door behind them.

Once they had sandwiched themselves into the two-door MG sports car, Sharon drove to the Shire Horse near the village of Woolley Green. There were several automobiles parked outside. "I hope there will be room," Sharon said.

"We'll make room." Linda got her legs out the door.

Inside the Shire Horse, they discovered they were the first to arrive. With the help of a delicate waitress, they were able to gather chairs and tables together in time for the arrival of the rest of the party.

Sharon was sipping a cup of coffee when Ernie arrived with a red-head named Etta who was taller than he and seemed to add a layer of polish to the man who was smartly dressed in his uniform.

Michael stepped inside the front door. Sharon stood up, met him at the end of the table, and drew him close. He smelled of soap and wool. She held his hand as they sat down together.

Edgar and Walter arrived next and stood cap in hand as they looked around the room. Sharon waved, and they sat down across the table.

"Have any trouble finding the place?" Sharon asked.

Edgar looked left and right. "Not really."

Walter smiled. "Edgar's nervous because he leaves tomorrow and he's never been to Italy before."

"I've heard that the Red Tails are making a substantial reputation for themselves," Michael said.

Edgar nodded.

Sharon watched the expression on Linda's face when Milton walked in. Linda's eyes brightened and a smile came automatically. *She really likes this guy.*

With Milton's arrival, the conversation turned to flying, missing home, and more flying. The awkwardness of the conversations faded, laughter began to dominate, and the food arrived.

So did half a dozen American soldiers, each with an airborne eagle on one shoulder and a red sash on the other. One of them had an arm in a sling. A couple of the others walked with pronounced limps. Another had yellow and purple bruising on one side of his face. He stopped when he saw the people at Linda's table. He frowned before following his comrades and taking a seat at a table behind Walter and Edgar. There was a loud scraping of chairs and combat boots.

Sharon looked at Michael and leaned in close to his ear. "Are those the paratroopers who were nearly wiped out by Monty's Market Garden plan?" Michael gave her a warning glance and nodded.

Fifteen minutes later, Sharon looked around the table. Linda and Milton sat shoulder to shoulder. Etta caressed the side of Ernie's face, and he blushed. Walter told another funny story about Edgar as a little boy in Mississippi who was always getting into trouble from telling the truth. She felt Michael's hand on her shoulder. Laughter erupted when Walter got to the punchline. *Perfect. This is wonderful. It's so nice to be able to say goodbye to someone when he's alive to hear it. I haven't felt happily normal like this in months.*

Five minutes later, she saw Edgar sit up straighter. She sensed the tension in the room and turned.

Edwin Beck stood just inside the door. He took off his white MP helmet and sat down at a table near the door. Sharon looked at Walter, who had stopped laughing. The voices of the American paratroopers got louder as the alcohol began to work its dark magic. The soldier with the bruised face raised his glass and said, "Here's to fuckin' Monty's plan. Piss poor planning: our guts, his gory glory!"

The men raised their glasses and shouted a chorus. "To Fuckin' Monty!"

Sharon looked over at Beck, who was smiling.

Michael glanced at his wife. "I need to get back to work early tomorrow morning." He looked at Edgar. "It's been a pleasure." He reached across the table to shake hands.

Walter glanced over at Beck. "Edgar has an early flight. We'd better be goin'."

Edgar pushed his chair back and inadvertently bumped into the soldier with the bruised face.

"Watch it, boy!" the paratrooper said.

Ernie turned to the paratrooper. "Back off!"

The paratrooper with the arm in a sling smiled. "Save it for the Nazis, George."

Sharon stood up and looked at Edgar. "Let's get some air."

She led the way outside as Milton, Michael, Walter, and Ernie reached into their pockets to pay the bill. Sharon, Linda, Edgar, and Etta stepped outside into the evening air, where the sun painted each brick, each leaf, a slightly richer hue.

Edgar said, "Thank you for dinner."

The paratrooper with the bruised face shoved the door open. It smashed against the wall, rebounded, and hit him in the face. He reached up with his hand and wiped at a bloody nose.

Sharon took Edgar's elbow. "Let's walk."

"Where I come from, you'd be called white trash!" the paratrooper said.

Edgar released Sharon's arm as he turned. The paratrooper balanced on drunken legs. He raised his fists. "Gonna teach you a lesson, blue gums!"

Another American came through the door. "George!"

George took a swing at Edgar, missed, and fell to his knees. Beck stood in the doorway. He reached for his pistol. "I'll shoot the next one who throws a punch."

Linda pointed at George. "*He's* the only one throwing punches."

George got to his feet and swung. He hit Edgar on the side of the face. Edgar reacted with a backhanded slap that sent George backwards into the other paratrooper.

There was an explosion. Sharon caught the stink of gunpowder and blood. Edgar reached up to his chest. Beck kept his pistol aimed at Edgar as he fell to the ground.

The paratrooper with the arm in a sling shouted, "Medic!"

Sharon watched Edgar roll onto his back. She dropped to her knees beside him. His eyes stared at her. A paratrooper knelt across from her and put his hand to Edgar's neck. She heard Michael say, "Put the gun away!"

The paratrooper kneeling across from her said, "No pulse."

For the next hour, Sharon watched the comings and goings with detachment.

The paratroopers gathered together and made coffee runs to sober up George, who vomited into the hedge at ten-minute intervals.

A squad of MPs arrived and began to talk with Beck.

Ernie and Walter wept openly and unashamedly. Etta did what she could to comfort them.

A military truck arrived, and two soldiers stepped out, put Edgar's body on a stretcher, slid it into the back of the truck, closed the tailgate, and drove away.

She felt Michael's arm around her shoulder, but only heard the occasional word that he said.

Linda sat at an outside table next to Milton. She leaned forward with her hands on her knees, and he rubbed her back.

A drab green Buick drove up. There was a single white star on the door. The driver climbed out and opened the rear door. A colonel stepped out. His hair was cut short. He placed a peaked cap on his head. He marched to the gathering of MPs. "What happened?" he asked.

"There was a fight," the senior MP replied. "Beck told them to stop or he would shoot. The coloured soldier didn't stop. Beck fired."

"That's it?"

The MPs nodded.

"Carry on." The colonel turned and returned to the staff car.

Sharon felt her rage detonate. "You!" She pointed at the colonel and ran to intercept him.

The colonel stopped, turned, and glared.

Sharon closed the gap to less than three feet. She read his name-tag: WILSON. "Colonel Wilson! Edgar Washington was unarmed. He was shot and killed in cold blood. What are you going to do about it?"

"Who the hell are you?" Wilson looked down his nose at her.

"Flight Captain Lacey." Sharon stepped closer so that there was only a foot between them.

Colonel Wilson smiled at her. "Well, Flight Captain Lacey, this is what I'm gonna do. There's a war on. It's not gonna stop because some coloured boy got himself shot!" He turned his back to her and climbed into the Buick. The driver closed the door, and Sharon watched them drive away.

CHAPTER 15
[SATURDAY, OCTOBER 21, 1944]

"Any news?" Ernie sat with his arms across his chest. A cup of coffee steamed on the table in front of him. He leaned back in a chair in a corner of the White Waltham dispersal hut.

Sharon sat down across from him with her coffee and a sandwich wrapped in wax paper. "Some."

Ernie looked at the black under his fingernails and hid them under the table. Then he leaned forward, causing the front legs of his chair to hit the floor. He lifted the coffee cup to his lips, sipped, put the cup down, then hid his hand under the table.

"Michael's been working on it from his end, and I should hear from him later today. I've made a series of phone calls. I have to check with Mother to see if there were any other replies while I was away doing that delivery." She lifted the folded triangles of wax paper and flipped the sandwich over.

"Other replies?" Ernie took his left hand up from under the table for another sip.

"So far I've been told that the Americans are our allies, and since it involves their personnel, it's their issue to deal with." Sharon looked at the sandwich and wondered where her appetite had gone.

"There a Lacey here? I've got a replacement for you!" The American voice boomed off the walls, causing every head in the room to turn. An MP stood at the door. As he moved inside, Walter Coleman followed behind.

Sharon stood up. "I'm Lacey."

The MP held out an envelope. "Colonel Wilson has sent you a replacement."

"Wally?" Sharon waited for Walter to meet her gaze. "You okay with this?"

Walter nodded, then looked sideways at the MP.

"Thank you, Sergeant." Sharon reached out and took the envelope. "Join us for coffee, Wally?" She walked over, fetched a cup of coffee, and turned. "Are you hungry, Wally?" She ignored the stone faces of the MP and Lady Ginette.

And for the first time in months, Sharon felt clarity. *From now on, I'm going to run this place the way it needs to be run. I don't care if there's a war on. You bigoted bastards can go to hell!*

CHAPTER 16
[SATURDAY, NOVEMBER 11, 1944]

"Priority delivery." Mother handed Sharon the chit. "617 Squadron. They need another of those modified Lancasters."

Sharon looked at the piece of paper. "Lossiemouth?"

"Almost as far north in Scotland as you can go." Mother smiled. "Think of it as a small vacation."

Sharon looked at the empty dispersal hut. "Everyone is off on a trip?"

"One of our busy days." Mother smiled at his little joke. Every day had become a busy day.

Half an hour later, Sharon found herself in the back seat of an elegant, lumbering de Havilland Rapide. The biplane always reminded her of a dragonfly. She sat and watched the walled fields and gentle hills amble by beneath as they flew north and west to the Avro Factory at Chadderton. Its massive rectangle of attached buildings was visible from at least twenty miles out.

Thirty minutes later, Sharon was hefting her gear through the back door of the Lancaster as she maneuvered her way along the obstacle course leading to the cockpit. A mechanic followed her inside and waited while she got herself settled in the pilot's seat.

"I expect you'll find this one is lighter than the others you've flown. The mid-upper turret has been removed, and so has some of the armour." He handed her the paperwork, she signed off, and he made his way out the back. She began her preflight checks. After finishing, she looked up through the canopy that was a greenhouse of Perspex. It allowed the sunshine to warm this autumn day.

She looked out her side of the canopy and slid open the side window when she spotted the mechanic near the nose of the Lancaster. She said, "Clear!" then began the process of starting each of the four massive Merlin engines.

Within ten minutes, she was headed north again, this time to the west coast of Scotland.

Sharon felt herself easing into the familiar routine of checking the sky for other aircraft with momentary glances at the instruments to ensure that all was well with the Lancaster.

When Glasgow was on her left and the North Sea on her right, a routine check of her gauges revealed a potential problem: the starboard engine on the inside was running hot. She looked right and saw the upper wing behind the engine was slick with a sheen of oil.

She checked the engine's oil pressure gauge. It was lower than the pressure on the other three engines. *I'm about an hour from Inverness. Do I land at Glasgow or carry on?*

She took another glance at the gauges for the starboard engine. The temperature gauge nudged into the red. The oil pressure continued its gradual drop that promised to end at zero.

Sharon took a long, slow breath to calm her nerves and began to shut down the engine before it could overheat and catch fire. She feathered the prop and stopped the oil-starved engine.

By the time she had dealt with the emergency, Glasgow was out of sight and behind her. The Lancaster seemed quite content flying on three engines, and she kept a close eye on the gauges for the remaining engines. *If I lose another one, I'm definitely going to have to find a place set down right away.*

Her eyes continued to sweep the horizon and check the gauges, sweep the horizon and check the gauges, sweep the horizon and check the gauges for the next forty-five minutes. She spotted the familiar tongue of land sticking out into the North Sea. Then she recognized the lopsided cross of RAF Lossiemouth's runways. *This baby is running just fine; no need to get on the radio. Jerry will be listening in.* She throttled back and began her pre-landing checklist.

She dropped the first stage of flaps, adjusted the controls and began to sweat as the Lancaster made her earn her pay for the second time that day. Sharon checked the circuit for other aircraft, saw none, and decided the best option at this point was to use a long, straight approach. She lowered the landing gear. The radio crackled in her ears: "Lancaster on long finals. Are you declaring an emergency?"

The controller must have spotted the feathered prop. She flicked the send switch. "Negative."

She concentrated on the landing. *You really don't want the excitement of doing a touch-and-go on three engines.*

The Lancaster touched down on its main gear. Sharon kept the tail up, then lowered it gently and was relieved that the tail wheel hadn't decided it was time to wobble. A wobbling tail wheel was a decidedly unpleasant experience in a Lancaster. It made the ship shudder from stem to stern.

Using the outboard engines and brakes, she taxied to the largest hangar and shut down. After she finished her checks, she raised her head to see that the Lancaster was surrounded by a quartet of vehicles.

When she opened the rear door, a hand was waiting to help her exit the aircraft. A man in uniform with short dark hair and a long slender face stood next to a Jeep and waved her over. As she approached the man, she heard a voice say, "That's not Lady Gannet!"

Sharon took a closer look at the man next to the Jeep. *He's a Wing Commander. What is going on here?*

The man held out his hand. "Willy Tate."

She hoisted her parachute and bag to her left shoulder and took his hand. "Sharon Lacey."

"The controller spotted the dead engine and thought it best to send out the crash crew." He released her hand and walked over nearer to the starboard wing. "It appears that you have an oil leak."

"The pressure was dropping and the temperature rose. So I shut it down. What's all the fuss about?"

Tate watched as the crash vehicles started up and left. A man in blue coveralls walked out of the hangar and looked at Tate, who said, "The starboard inner has an oil leak. Is it possible for this one to be ready for tomorrow?"

"We'll see what we can do, sir."

Tate turned to Sharon. "Can I give you a lift to the NAFFI wagon?"

Sharon nodded. "I'd still like to know what all the fuss was about. I didn't declare an emergency."

Tate talked as they walked to the Jeep. "Six months ago, and before my time, an ATA pilot had a problem with her fuel cocks. One of her engines shut down due to fuel starvation. It turned out that she'd inadvertently shut off the fuel to one of the engines."

Sharon put her parachute and bag in the back of the Jeep.

"She landed safely and she stopped over there." Tate pointed to the end of the runway.

Sharon climbed into the Jeep.

Tate sat behind the wheel and hit the starter. "The pilot was in such a state that she had to be carried off the Anson, put on a stretcher, and taken in an ambulance to the infirmary. A series of dramatic events ensued which were, apparently, quite spectacular."

Sharon held on as he shifted up through the gears.

"After she left, the Group Commander received a number of calls from well-placed individuals voicing their concern that we hadn't taken the pilot's plight seriously enough. And after that, we were instructed to make sure that nothing like that ever happened again." Tate turned onto a road running between two hangars. "So, when the controller heard a woman's voice and saw that she piloted a Lancaster with one of its engines out, he called for the crash crew just to be on the safe side."

"Lady Gannet?" Sharon asked.

"Yes, that's her nickname. Apparently, she was quite big-breasted and sounded remarkably like a squawking bird, so she's become notorious hereabouts." Tate turned left, pulled up in at the NAAFI wagon, and stopped.

"Lady Gannet? Lady Ginette Elam?" Sharon climbed out of the Jeep.

"So I've been told." Tate turned the engine off and followed Sharon to the grey truck with its open side hatch and rear doors. Two pilots turned and saluted Tate. He returned their greetings.

"Thank you for your kindness," Sharon said.

"A distinct pleasure for me. My fiancée is a WAAF. You're a bit of a legend with them. They say you're an ace." Tate put a hand on the side of the NAFFI truck. "What do you take in your coffee?"

Sharon smiled. "Cream and sugar, please."

CHAPTER 17
[SUNDAY, NOVEMBER 26, 1944]

Sharon looked at the backs of her hands. *They're black from the fire!* She turned them over and saw that the palms were pink.

Her nose filled with the stink of burning hair, gasoline, and flesh. She stepped over the body of a German pilot who stared up at her with dead eyes. *He's only eighteen or nineteen.* There were more bodies to step over. All but one wore a flight helmet. Most wore tan flight suits. A few wore black leather jackets. One face had the top of its skull blown off. The eyes were gone, but the nose and the mouth remained. Sharon stepped over another body, then looked ahead.

The flames framed a pathway to escape. She began to walk along the corridor. The heat made it feel like her clothing was about to burst into flame.

Sharon looked up. Beck stood there with his sidearm aimed at her chest. She covered her eyes when she saw the muzzle flash.

"Sharon!"

She felt someone sitting next to her.

"Sharon!" Linda said.

"What?"

"You're having a nightmare. You woke me up! It's three o'clock in the bloody morning!"

"This came for you." Mother handed her a letter. "It came last evening, and I wasn't here when you returned." He looked outside at the inky blackness of the early morning and smelled the threat of rain.

"Thank you." The letter was from Sir Gerard d'Erlanger. Sharon flipped the envelope over and stuck a fingernail under the flap. She opened the letter, grabbed a cup of coffee, and sat down at an empty table in an empty room.

DEAR FLIGHT CAPTAIN SHARON LACEY,

THIS IS IN RESPONSE TO YOUR LETTER OF OCTOBER 22ND, 1944.

REPEATED ATTEMPTS HAVE BEEN MADE BY THIS OFFICE TO GATHER INFORMATION CONCERNING THE EVENTS SURROUNDING THE DEATH OF UNITED STATES AIR FORCE AIRMAN EDGAR WASHINGTON. ENQUIRIES HAVE BEEN MADE AT THE HIGHEST LEVELS, AND TO NO AVAIL.

THE RESPONSIBILITY FOR MAKING DECISIONS AS TO THE CONDUCT OF SERGEANT EDWIN BECK LIES WITH THE REPRESENTATIVES OF THE UNITED STATES. THOSE REPRESENTATIVES HAVE STEADFASTLY VOICED THE OPINION THAT THIS MATTER WILL BE DEALT WITH THROUGH UNITED STATES MILITARY PROTOCOLS. THEIR OFFICIAL POSITION IS THAT AIRMAN WASHINGTON WAS WARNED OF THE CONSEQUENCES OF HIS ACTIONS AND CHOSE TO DISREGARD SAID WARNING. AS A RESULT, NO ACTION WILL BE TAKEN AGAINST SERGEANT BECK.

SINCE WE ARE AT WAR AND THE UNITED STATES IS AN ALLY TO GREAT BRITAIN, BRITISH AUTHORITIES ARE RELUCTANT TO TAKE UNILATERAL ACTION IN THIS MATTER.

SINCERELY YOURS,
SIR GERARD D'ERLANGER

Sharon inhaled to quell her anger, folded the letter, and slipped it back inside the envelope. She took her time finishing her coffee.

Mother watched her from behind the counter. The phone sat next to him. It was unusually silent even for this early in the morning.

Sharon got up, poured Mother a cup of tea, and walked over to his counter. "Here you go. Looks like we might not be doing much flying today."

"Thank you." Mother slid the cup a little closer to inhale the aroma.

"Don't worry, I won't make fetching your tea a habit." Sharon grabbed an umbrella, stuffed the letter inside her flight suit, and stepped outside. She popped open the umbrella and walked to the hangar. The rain spattered against the drumlike surface protecting her head and shoulders.

The light from inside the hangar spilled out the open front door, where a pair of Ansons, the Storch, and a Rapide sat. The light was a breach of blackout regulations, but no one was going to attack in this weather.

She spotted Walter first. He wore a pair of grey coveralls and was looking along the shelves along the near wall where oil and other fluids were stored. He spotted Sharon, smiled, and held up a finger.

Ernie was standing on a wooden crate turned upside down. His legs and backside were visible, but the rest of him was behind the hood of a black Austin that Sharon recognized as Mother's.

"Engine oil will work, won't it?" Walter held up a quart can of oil for effect.

"How many times do I have to fuckin' tell you that you can't use motor oil for brake fluid! It eats away at the rubber seals and then the brakes fail." Ernie backed out from under the hood, looked to his left, and blushed.

Walter laughed. Sharon smiled. Ernie stepped off the crate, pulled a rag from his back pocket, and wiped his hands. Sharon spun the umbrella so that the water flew off. Then she set it down and pulled the envelope from a pocket in her flight suit. "I finally got a reply."

Ernie moved closer. Walter tipped back his cap and leaned against the bench. "What's it say?" Ernie asked.

"You want to read it?" Sharon held it out.

Walter reached for the letter, wiped his right hand on the side of his coveralls, and pulled the letter from its envelope. Ernie and Sharon studied his expression as he read. He finished, looked at Sharon, and handed the letter back. Sharon offered it to Ernie.

"What's it say?" Ernie asked, then saw Walter shake his head. "Son of a bitch."

"You know, it's funny." Walter crossed his arms in front of his chest. "Nobody at the base has any use for Beck. And there's been lots of talk about what happened to Edgar. Some say he should have stopped fighting. But most say it was Beck making a point."

"About what?" Sharon asked.

"About people like me and Edgar getting above ourselves." Walter pointed at his chest for emphasis.

Sharon shook her head and looked at the floor. She remembered Edgar pushing her to the ground the moment before the V-1 buzz bomb exploded in a nearby field. "I miss him."

Walter looked at the floor, then looked out into the darkness at the sound of an approaching vehicle. A black Humber with four doors and elegant front fenders pulled up in front of the open hangar door. Sharon saw Michael at the wheel. There was something in his expression that made her put her hand to her throat.

Michael left the engine running as he climbed out of the car and crossed the line of wet into the dry shelter of the hangar. He nodded at Walter and Ernie.

"What's happened?" Sharon asked. "Is Sean all right?"

"It's not Sean; it's my father." Michael stood there until she came to him. She wrapped her arms around his shoulders. He tucked his face into the crook of her neck.

It took almost half an hour and two cups of coffee before Michael could tell them what happened. He stared at his half-full coffee mug while he sat on a toolbox. The others sat on upturned crates and pails.

"I got news this morning. His body was identified. A rocket hit Woolworth's in London. Over five hundred people were killed. Apparently, my father was in there doing some Christmas shopping." Michael looked up at Sharon. "It was one of those quirks he had. He loved to shop to clear his mind."

"You said a rocket killed him," Sharon said.

"Another of Hitler's vengeance weapons. A V-2. We've known about them for some time. So far, they're too fast to shoot down. They have to be destroyed at their source." Michael turned his cup upside down and watched the remaining coffee drip onto the floor. "I have to tell Honeysuckle and Linda."

"The weather's clearing, and Church Fenton needs a Mosquito night fighter." Mother handed the chit to Sharon. "It'll be a bit cramped for the three of you, but this will get you close to home. The Anson has room and is waiting to ferry you to Church Fenton. If you leave now, you'll be there before dark."

Sharon took the chit and saw that they were headed first for Hatfield, situated south and east of London. *If we're lucky, we'll be in Church Fenton by midnight.* "Thanks, Mother. Will you keep an eye on things for me?"

"Don't you worry. We've got this place running so it will operate whether we're here or not." He dropped his voice and leaned closer. "I'll keep Lady Gannet from getting too puffed up with herself."

"How did you hear about Lossiemouth?" Sharon asked.

"You're referring to her command performance and your uneventful emergency landing? It's my business to know what goes on with all of my pilots. My friend Robert has an extensive intelligence network." Mother smiled and waved her out of the door.

Sharon found Michael and Linda in the hangar. They were chatting with a man who weighed at least twice as much as she did. She was pleased to see he had a better-fitting tan flight suit than she'd seen him wearing the last time. Douglas, one of the Anson taxi pilots, turned to her and smiled from under a pair of eyebrows badly in need of a shearing. "Hello, Sharon. We need to be on our way to make Hatfield before nightfall." His voice was part growl, part laughter.

"Douglas. Thank you for giving us a ride on such short notice. How are the boys?" Sharon asked.

Michael reached down to help Linda up.

"The twins are fifteen. I just hope this war'll be over before they're called upon." Douglas maneuvered his way to the Anson. He danced delicately over a puddle. "Watch your step. Just gave the old girl a cleaning inside and out." He opened the side door of the aircraft and squeezed inside.

Michael followed Linda and Sharon.

Sharon sat down. She saw that her sister-in-law's face was aged with grief. She touched Linda on the knee. Linda made eye contact for about thirty seconds and unsuccessfully attempted a smile.

They were in the air soon after. The sun was low in the sky. Leaf-less trees left long fingers of shadow on the ground.

Sharon thought about Harry and the way he'd warned her to stay away from London. Then she remembered the smell of his wool suit as he'd walked beside her. She closed her eyes and remembered how her arm was tucked through the crook of his elbow at her wedding. She thought about how they'd walked up the aisle of the church to Michael and the minister waiting at the altar. And how Harry had said, "It's an honour to stand in for your father, Patrick."

Linda, Michael, and Sharon sat cocooned within their memories until Douglas throttled back. Sharon watched him crank the wheels down. Then she studied the dance of his massive fingers on the throt-tle and the controls. He held the wheels off of the ground as long as possible until they skipped over the surface of the runway. Five min-utes later, they watched him take off.

"Whatcher here for?" The man's voice made the three of them turn. He wore a leather vest over a sparkling pair of coveralls. Even his boots shone. He wore sergeant stripes on his sleeve.

Sharon reached into the breast pocket of her flight suit and pulled out the delivery chit. The man took the chit and studied it. Sharon noticed that his fingernails were clean and his face was clean-shaven, except for a precisely trimmed moustache.

"This is only for one aircraft," the sergeant said.

"That's correct," Sharon said.

"There are three of you." He looked at them, pointed at each in turn, and crossed his arms. "Against regulations to take passengers along."

Sharon looked at Michael, who stared at the sergeant, then reached for his inside jacket pocket. He pulled out his identification and stuck it in front of the sergeant's nose.

The sergeant stepped closer, looked at the document, and looked at Michael before he said, "Romeo Sierra is nearly ready. The aircraft is fully operational. That means you. . ." He pointed a finger at Sharon. ". . .will keep your finger away from the arming switch and the firing button."

Linda opened her mouth to speak. Sharon saw that her friend's face was red. Michael gripped his sister's elbow. Sharon shook her head, turned, walked away, and did her walk around the aircraft. *That pompous sergeant will get an earful if he's not careful.*

After the exterior check, Sharon was the first to climb through the Mosquito's floor hatch. Michael followed and settled himself into the observer's chair. Linda sat on his knee.

The sergeant peered up at them as Sharon began her preflight checks.

The sergeant pointed at Linda. "You keep your fingers off of the radar set!"

Linda looked down at him, pulled on a pair of headphones, switched on the radar set, and said, "Shut the fucking hatch!"

Sharon slid open the side window. "Clear!"

The propeller on her side began to roll over.

The sergeant's face disappeared and the hatch shut.

Sharon soon had both engines running smoothly. She nodded at her husband and her friend, then taxied out to the end of the runway.

Sharon felt the familiar thrill when she had the runway lined up and the power of the Merlin engines in her hands. She opened the throttles. The Mosquito accelerated. They were airborne in less than a minute. She retracted the undercarriage and headed north and west into the blackness of a wartime sky where no lights shone up from the ground. There was only the ghostly glow of the instruments and engine exhausts.

When she had the aircraft trimmed for level flight, she turned to Linda, who continued to fiddle with the radar set. Sharon tapped her friend on the shoulder, smiled, and waggled her finger. Linda smiled back.

Sharon took them north and around the western side of London. Michael put his hand on her shoulder. She turned to him and he nodded.

Less than an hour later, they flew past Manchester. Sharon began a gradual descent for Church Fenton. She saw the runway lights up ahead and began to plan her approach. She reached for the microphone. "Romeo Sierra joining downwind."

"Romeo Sierra," said the controller. "You are number two."

Sharon felt a tap on her elbow. She saw that Linda was pointing at the radar screen and holding up three fingers. Sharon looked ahead to see if she could spot the other aircraft in the circuit. She pressed the microphone. "This is Romeo Sierra. Confirm we are number two."

"Confirmed," came the reply. "You are number two."

Sharon looked at Linda, who shook her head and held up three fingers.

"Romeo Sierra here. My radar operator has two aircraft ahead of us in the circuit." Sharon looked for the arming switch and flicked it to the on position.

"Romeo Sierra, the second aircraft is a bandit! You are cleared to engage."

Sharon was already on the throttles. The Merlins thrummed as they went to full power.

Linda used her hand to signal that the bandit was directly ahead.

Sharon felt the throttle in one hand, the control stick in the other, and her feet on the pedals. She looked ahead into the black and searched for any hint of the enemy night fighter. Her mind cleared itself of all distractions. Her index finger hovered over the button that would fire the four cannons under her feet.

Michael touched her shoulder and pointed. Sharon spotted the subtle glow of a pair of engine exhausts just ahead and slightly above. She closed on the fighter until they were within what she estimated to be one hundred yards.

She coordinated ailerons and rudder until the gun sight was aligned on one of the glowing exhausts. She pressed the trigger. The pounding of the cannons was telegraphed though the soles of her flying boots. Cannon shells exploded along the wing and nacelle of the enemy fighter. The engine exploded into flame.

In the light of the flash, she recognized the silhouette as a Junkers 88. She lined up the nose of the Mosquito on the Junker's other engine and fired.

She missed as the Nazi fighter turned left.

Sharon turned with the Junkers, led the enemy fighter, and fired.

Her cannon shells exploded along the opposite wing and the second engine began to trail flames. She saw the Nazi pilot drop his wheels.

He has no choice but to land at Church Fenton. She throttled back to stay on his tail just in case.

She followed him and watched him touch down at the end of the runway. Sharon peeled off to the right, turned speed into altitude, and began her landing checks. She touched the microphone button. "Romeo Sierra cleared to land?"

"Romeo Sierra number one in the circuit. Orbit at angels one thousand so that we can get Jerry off the runway and check for debris. By the way, that was quite a display."

Sharon and Linda kept their eyes open in case the Junkers was not alone. After receiving clearance, she landed beyond where the Junkers had rolled to a stop. A few minutes later, she parked the Mosquito in front of a hangar and shut the engines down.

Linda was the first to climb through the hatch. Michael followed and waited under the nose of the night fighter for Sharon. The three of them stood under the Mosquito as a group of mechanics gathered around the nose of the aircraft where it was parked just outside the hangar door. They looked across the field at the Junkers. A fire crew finished extinguishing the flames. One mechanic asked, "Anyone see what happened?"

A pair of airmen came around the side of the hangar. Both were wearing flight suits. One was still wearing his helmet while the blonde one carried his gear in his hand. The blonde looked at Michael. "You shot that Junkers right off our tail! Mind if we treat you to a pint?"

Michael turned to Sharon and winked. "Will you throw in a ride to the mess and a cup of coffee?"

The five of them crammed into an ancient Austin. It backfired most of the way to the mess, where a dozen other pilots raised their glasses when Michael greeted them.

Michael was led to a table where he sat down with Sharon and Linda. Cups of coffee appeared before them. Sharon lifted her cup to her nose. She caught the sweet scent of rum mixed in with the coffee, then took a sip.

The door to the mess opened. All attention turned toward the new arrivals. A German Luftwaffe pilot, wearing a blue peaked cap, black leather jacket, and blue pants stepped into the room. His hands were handcuffed in front of him. Another Luftwaffe airman wearing a leather flying helmet and a tan flight suit followed him. This man looked around the room before he raised his handcuffed hands to remove his flying helmet. A red-capped military policeman followed the pair.

Sharon looked at Linda, who watched the German airmen. Linda turned to Sharon. "They killed your father and mine. Why didn't you kill them?"

Sharon opened her mouth to answer, but stopped. *I'm tired of the killing.*

A deep voice said, "Raise your glasses to the man who saved our arses!" Sharon recognized the speaker as the blonde pilot of the Mosquito who had been number one in the circuit and was within seconds of being killed. She watched Michael stand. He pulled his chair back and stood on it.

"Cheers!" the blonde pilot said.

Michael raised his cup with his right hand, then held up his open left hand for quiet. The room grew silent.

"Raise your glasses to Sharon the pilot and Linda the radar operator who shot down the 88. I was only a passenger!" He pointed at his wife and sister and bowed.

After a momentary silence, the Luftwaffe pilot spoke up: "Erzähl mir nicht solche Scheiße!"

"Bloody hell!" said the blonde RAF pilot. "That was an amazing bit of flying."

The Luftwaffe airman in the tan flight suit said, "Forgive my pilot's rudeness. We owe you for our lives. You deliberately shot out our engines, yes?" He looked at Sharon and Linda.

Sharon nodded. "Yes."

"Thank you."

CHAPTER 18

[MONDAY, NOVEMBER 27, 1944]

"We're here." Michael's hand was on Sharon's shoulder.

She sat up and opened her eyes. The morning sky was orange, red, and pink. The car was stopped in front of Townsend Farm.

They thanked the driver and stumbled out of the Austin. He shifted into gear, and the car putt-putted away.

Sharon tucked her hand inside of Michael's elbow. *I wonder what he will say to Honeysuckle?*

They found Michael and Linda's mother in the kitchen. When Sharon stepped through the door, she saw Honeysuckle's eyes and realized that the woman already knew.

Michael wrapped his arms around her. She tucked her head up against his neck and held her son tight. "Did he suffer?"

"I don't think so. Those rockets hit before the people on the ground can hear them. The noise comes after." Michael sat her down and pulled up a chair to sit next to her. Linda brought another chair to sit on the other side of her mother.

"I've been expecting you," Honeysuckle said.

"The weather held us up. Then Sharon and Linda shot down a Luftwaffe night fighter." Michael looked across at his sister. "Was that last night or this morning?"

Probably better if we don't answer that, Sharon thought.

"Does it matter?" Linda asked.

"Does it matter?!" Honeysuckle stood up. "The three of you together in one airplane, dogfighting! Does it matter? We just lost Harry, and now you tell me that you went out of your way to get into a dogfight? What would Sean and I do if you were shot down?"

"Actually, we weren't in any danger." Michael pointed at his sister and his wife. "And neither was the crew of the Junkers that was shot down. Sharon was very careful to hit only the engines. The radar operator was kind enough to thank Sharon. He actually said, 'We owe you for our lives.'"

Honeysuckle looked at her son. "You really are telling me the truth, aren't you?"

Michael nodded.

"I don't know what I'd do if I lost the three of you as well." Honeysuckle moved around the kitchen. "I told myself that if we could all survive this war. That it would be okay. That we could get back to our lives after the war. Then Harry's friend called to offer his condolences. That Harry was killed in Woolworth's. Can you imagine? He was killed because I asked him to pick up a few things for Christmas. Sometimes I think I'll go mad!"

"So why didn't you kill those Nazis? They killed my father. They killed your father." Linda gave Sharon a hard look.

"I killed fifteen men the day my father was killed. It didn't make me feel any better. Now I think the whole thing, this entire war, has been a huge waste." Sharon looked back at her sister-in-law.

"The crew of that Mosquito seemed pretty happy with the pair of you. They had no idea Jerry was on their tail. They were meat on the table. If you hadn't been on the radar set, they would have been killed." Michael put his arm around his sister's shoulder.

Linda pushed him away and smiled. The anger died in her eyes as she looked at her mother, then at Sharon.

"It's good to see you smile." Honeysuckle touched Linda's hand.

Sean stepped into the kitchen. "What's going on?" He wore a brown work shirt and pants.

"We just got here." Sharon got up to give him a hug. She looked over her shoulder at Honeysuckle.

"I already know about Harry," Sean said.

"I have to go into Ilkley." Michael stood over Sharon where she had fallen asleep on the couch.

Sharon lifted the blanket, sat up, stood, and began to fold the quilt as she gathered her thoughts. She looked out the window. *It looks to be about midday.*

"Sean said he would drive. I thought I'd let Mother and Linda sleep." Michael handed her a cup of coffee.

She eyed him warily. "Thank you."

He smiled. "Don't get used to it."

Sharon took a sip and closed her eyes. *Tastes like home.*

Sean stepped into the living room and looked at his sister. "You're up. Can we go?"

Michael smiled at Sharon as if to say, "He loves to drive and any excuse will do."

Ten minutes later, she sat in the back seat of the Austin while Sean and Michael sat up front. *It's hard to believe that less than twelve hours ago, I was shooting down a Junkers.* Sharon looked out of the window at a flock of blackbirds gathered in the naked, crooked limbs of an oak.

"Where do I drop you?" Sean asked as he shifted up a gear.

The road opened up and the sun shone on the side of her brother's face. *He's got hair growing on his cheek.* She felt an ache in her chest. *I hope the war will be over before he's old enough to fight.*

"I need to see the undertaker to make arrangements." Michael turned to look at Sharon. "Do you want to accompany me to the lawyer afterward?"

"Sean, will you come with me?" Sharon watched her brother's shoulders.

"All right," Sean said with a shrug.

"Then I'll meet you there afterward." Michael stared out the window and continued to do so in silence until Sean stopped in front of the undertakers.

Minutes later, Sean parked alongside a three-storey brick building near the centre of town.

They both stepped out. Sean followed her to the oak and glass door etched with McGregor and Son. She opened the door and stopped. A brown-haired woman in a white blouse looked up and stopped typing. The woman was Sharon's age, but taller and stockier. She smiled.

"I'm Sharon Lacey, ummm, Townsend. This is my brother Sean." Sharon felt Sean brush against her shoulder as he shut the door behind them.

"Of course you are." The woman got up, smoothed her pleated tan wool skirt, then walked around to the front of her desk. She held out her hand. "Rosemary Lewis. I'll let Mr. McGregor know that you're here." She released Sharon's hand and went to another oak door with opaque glass in the upper half. Rosemary tapped on the glass and opened the door. "Sharon Lacey-Townsend and brother to see you."

"Send them in." Rupert's voice carried into the outside room.

Rosemary held the door open as Sharon and Sean went inside. The door clicked shut behind them.

Rupert walked around the corner of the desk. He held out his hand. "My sympathies."

Sharon shook his hand. "It was a shock. I don't think it's really sunk in yet."

"Sit down, please. Would you like coffee or tea?" Rupert waited until they sat down in the chairs across from the desk.

Sharon looked at Sean. He shrugged. She looked at Rupert in his immaculate navy blue suit, white shirt, and blue tie. "If you're having coffee, we'd like some too, please."

There was the creak of leather and metal from his artificial leg as he went to the door. "Rosemary, would you mind bringing us all a coffee?" He closed the door and went back to his desk.

"How did you hear about Harry?" Sharon looked around at the books on shelves and a row of filing cabinets against the other wall.

"Harry? Harry Townsend?" Rupert stared at Sharon as he went to the side of his desk.

Sharon saw him do a mental replay of their conversation. She thought, *Oh no. Not more bad news!*

"I wasn't referring to Harry. I was referring to your grandmother. I meant Cornelia." Rupert looked from Sharon to Sean.

"Harry was killed on Saturday. He was at Woolworths in London on the twenty-fifth."

Rupert shook his head. "I'm afraid I'm going to add to your grief. Cornelia died on the eleventh of November."

"I wasn't notified?" Sharon leaned forward.

"I found out quite by chance. On the fourteenth, Rosemary learned that your grandmother had been buried in the cemetery." Rupert sat down is his leather chair.

"Marmaduke." Sean made no attempt to disguise the anger in his voice.

"I had a letter posted to notify you," Rupert said.

"It will probably be waiting for me when I get back." Sharon tried to think, but felt as if her brain was working in slow motion.

"I would recommend that we begin the process of probating the will," Rupert said.

Sharon looked at him for a full thirty seconds. "How long will that take?"

"Most probably a year." Rupert turned his eyes to Sean.

Sharon heard the crackle of paper. She turned to Sean, who was pulling a folded manila envelope from his jacket pocket.

"Harry was home at the end of October. He gave this to me to give to you the next time Sharon and I came to this office." He stood, leaned across the desk, and handed the envelope to Rupert.

The lawyer opened a drawer and pulled out a silver letter opener. He slit the top edge of the envelope, pulled out the contents, and began to read through what appeared to be a series of documents. He frowned. His eyes grew hard. He looked at Sharon, then at Sean. "These are quite extraordinary. I need to have Rosemary prepare some documents for you to sign to initiate the probating of the will. I also need to consider the import of these." He held up the papers he'd pulled from the envelope. "Could I impose upon you to return in one hour?"

He waited for a response.

"We'll be back in an hour." Sean took Sharon's arm and went outside. She looked at him as he said, "Come on. Let's get something to eat across the street. I'll keep an eye out for Michael."

Sean took her inside the pub and sat them near the window. He looked at his watch and ordered for them.

Sharon sat and stared out the window, watching people and vehicles amble past. *I thought I was handling it all. Harry being killed. Not being able to say goodbye to him. Now not being able to say goodbye to Cornelia.* She looked at the backs of her hands, half expecting to feel her mother's hands taking hold of her, offering her comfort.

Ten minutes later, a steak and kidney pie was put in front of her. She took a bite. It tasted like paste.

She didn't notice when Sean got up.

A minute later, Michael sat down beside her. She heard him ask, "What's the matter with her?"

"McGregor told her that Cornelia died," Sean said.

"Cornelia? When?"

"Two or three weeks ago."

Sharon felt Michael put his arm around her shoulder. "Sharon?"

She saw the concern in the lines across his forehead, but could think of nothing to say.

"McGregor wants us to go back in about half an hour," Sean said.

Sharon felt Michael move closer. "Would you like spot of whiskey?"

She turned to glare at him.

"At least that's an improvement over catatonia." Sean began to laugh.

Michael rubbed Sharon between the shoulders. She looked at her palms, brought them to her face, and began to weep.

Thirty minutes later, Sharon had washed her face with cold water before they went back to see the lawyer. She knew the aftermath of her grief was a stain on her face.

As the three of them entered the office, Rosemary said, "I've made coffee. Would you like some?"

"Yes, please," Michael said.

Rosemary got up at the same time as Sharon. The secretary poured coffee into a bone china cup and handed it to Sharon. Rosemary did the same for Michael and Sean.

Sharon added sugar and cream, then looked at Rosemary. "You'll join us, won't you?" Rosemary looked over her shoulder. "I'll tell him I insisted," Sharon said.

"Don't mind if I do." Rosemary poured another cup, sipped it black, and looked at Sharon. "You have no idea who I am, do you?"

Sharon held her cup near her chin. She could think of nothing to say by way of reply.

"Rosemary Lewis. Daughter-in-law to Margaret Lewis." Rosemary held the saucer and cup and waited.

Sharon tried to think. She remembered a rough woman in a two-door Morris van and the stink of chicken feathers. "How is your husband?"

"He's back from Italy. Healing up from shrapnel wounds. He'll be fine." Rosemary pointed at her chest. "That makes us related in a round-about way. Your mother was kind to Margaret. She never forgot it."

"How is Margaret?" *That's it! Rosemary's husband Bill is Uncle Marmaduke's illegitimate child!*

"Still selling chickens and milk in her Morris van. Happy that Bill is back and not likely to be called up again." Rosemary took another sip of coffee.

"You've been kind. Thank you." Sharon felt close to tears again.

"Margaret and Honeysuckle talk at least once a week. We're all very proud of you. We know what you've done. We know that Marmaduke has stayed safe at home, sitting on his fortune, while you, Linda, Harry, and Michael have been fighting for us. Everyone says your mother would be proud." Rosemary saw the tears in Sharon's eyes. "I'm sorry if I've upset you."

Sharon reached out with her left hand and touched Rosemary's arm. "Actually, you've made me feel much better."

"She shot down another one last night," Sean said. Sharon glared at him. "She always starts to perk up when she gets her wind up. She's furious that I've mentioned it." Sean smiled.

The door to Rupert McGregor's office opened. "Sorry for the delay." He held out his hand. "Michael. Good of you to come. My condolences."

They filed in, Rupert shut the door behind them, and creaked over to his desk. He put both hands on the arms of the chair and lowered himself into the chair. "These documents provided by Sean are remarkable." He looked up at Sean. "By the way, have you read them?"

Sean shook his head no and looked at his sister.

"Much of what I'm about to say falls under attorney-client privilege. Will anything we say be repeated outside of this room?"

Sharon looked at Michael, who smiled, and Sean, who shook his head. "Understood," she said.

"Apparently, Marmaduke Lacey and his wife were quite close to Norah Elam and Diana Mosley; both were interned in Holloway Prison." Rupert picked up one of the documents as if offering it into evidence.

"Father always said that Marmaduke had backed the wrong horse in this war," Michael said.

Rupert held up another document. "He also profited handsomely because of it. A very astute businessman. Being connected with the fascists before the war and profiting from it mightily from the safety of Lacey Manor will not sit well if word of this gets out."

"I want nothing to do with Marmaduke," Sharon said.

"And I'm sure he wants less to do with you. These documents, however, may assure you of a substantial inheritance. I believe an American might call it leverage." Rupert looked directly at Sharon, then lifted his artificial leg up off the floor, adjusted it, then dropped it with a thunk. "It will give me great satisfaction to see Marmaduke Lacey separated from a sizable portion of what he values most."

"What does he value most?" Sharon asked.

"Money and status, of course."

CHAPTER 19

"Antwerp has been under heavy V-2 rocket attack for the past two days." Petrie sat in the front seat of the Rolls-Royce. He barked rather than spoke, and Sharon was sure he was used to being obeyed. She'd noticed how the others at Harry's funeral had deferred to him. And how Michael didn't argue when Petrie announced that the three of them would ride east to Leeds in his car.

Sharon looked neither right nor left. Michael sat on one side and Linda on the other. They hadn't discussed the funeral. *I know they're both thinking that the coffin was a little light. The funeral director had advised they have a closed coffin, which I'm sure meant that there was very little of Harry left to bury.*

Petrie turned around to reveal a square jaw, grey, close-cut hair, and moustache. He looked at Sharon. "You're Lacey?"

Sharon nodded. "That's correct."

"Shooting that Junkers down without killing the crew provided us with some valuable intelligence. Good work." Petrie glanced at Linda.

Sharon cocked a thumb in Linda's direction. "She picked the Junkers up on radar."

"And I would have killed them." Linda continued to look out of the window.

"So you're the bloodthirsty type, are you, Miss Townsend?" Petrie didn't smile, but there was humour in his voice.

"The Nazis killed her father and mine." Linda met Petrie's gaze.

"And to those in the know, Lacey here is reported to have ten victories in the air." Petrie shifted his eyes from Linda to Sharon.

"You are very well-informed," Michael said.

"A necessity of my profession." Petrie turned to his driver. "We'll drop them off at RAF Leeds so they can catch their ride back to White Waltham." He turned to face the trio in the back seat. "That should have the three of you back in time for supper. It's certainly odd to have a group like you lot in the back seat of one car."

Sharon asked, "What do you mean?"

"Three people who have done remarkable things, yet will probably never have their work recognized in the papers or on the radio." Petrie faced forward and was quiet for the rest of the trip.

Douglas was waiting for them at the Leeds airport. As they settled in the cramped seats of the Anson, he said, "Mother got a high-priority call to pick up the three of you. What have you been up to this time? A meeting with ministers of state?"

Sharon looked out the window.

"My father's funeral," said Linda.

"Oh." Douglas turned and busied himself with starting the engines and operating the aircraft.

It was a quiet flight to White Waltham.

Sharon kept her mind occupied with thoughts of the operations of the airfield, personnel, and aircraft. On approach, she spotted a Jeep with a white star on the hood parked next to the hangar. She tried to see exactly what was happening, but was too far away.

After Douglas taxied up close to the hangar, she was the first out the door, and what she saw set her on quick boil.

Sergeant Beck stood toe to toe with Ernie, who only reached up to the MP's chin, but was not about to surrender any ground.

Douglas shut down the Anson's engines.

Sharon heard Beck say, "I've received a report that stolen United States property is in this hangar, and I intend to do a search."

Ernie's face reddened. "And I'm saying you're not going anywhere near my tools, you murdering bastard!"

Sharon closed the distance quickly while being careful not to run. "Sergeant?" Beck turned and put his hand on his holstered .45. "Shouldn't you be dealing with me?" She intentionally put Beck in the awkward position of being caught with Ernie behind him and her in front.

"Then I'm telling you I'm taking a look inside of this hangar." Beck looked down on her.

"Do you have a written request from Colonel Wilson?" Sharon moved closer to the sergeant and sensed that Michael, Linda, and Douglas were behind her.

Beck stepped sideways. "Not yet."

"Then I suggest that you get Wilson's written request, then make an appointment with me, and I will give the request the consideration it deserves." Sharon crossed her arms.

Beck opened the flap of his holstered automatic.

Sharon took a step closer. She got a whiff of cologne and alcohol and saw that the sergeant had a cut just under his chin.

The sergeant stepped sideways, walked to his Jeep, climbed inside, started the engine, released the clutch, and sprayed them with gravel as he accelerated away.

Sharon looked at Ernie, who was so enraged he was unable to speak. "Let me handle this," she said. She walked to dispersal and found Mother behind the counter.

"My condolences," Mother said.

She studied him. His grey hair had been roughly combed. *Good, there are no dark circles under his eyes.* "Anything new?"

"Besides a visit from that bastard who murdered Edgar?" Mother did not smile. "Any idea who told the good sergeant there was stolen US property in the hangar?" she asked.

Mother looked Sharon in the eye, then glanced over her shoulder in the direction of Lady Ginette, who was sitting at a table with three other pilots. Her loud laughter made talk momentarily impossible.

Mother focused on Sharon's eyes. "Our mechanic and a certain pilot had a difference of opinion two days back. Apparently, the pilot believes that people like you, me, and the mechanic need to learn to defer to our betters."

Sharon nodded. *Harry said I could handle her, but I have no idea what to do next. I know what to do in the air when there is an enemy, but here, on the ground, in this kind of situation, I'm at a loss.* She noticed Lady Ginette turn and glance at Mother. Ginette turned back around, and a moment later, laughter erupted at the table.

Sharon felt a sudden rage. She thought back to Molly Hume's isolation, then turned to Mother. "How many chits do you have waiting for deliveries?"

Mother fanned six chits. Sharon took them, walked over to Lady Ginette's table, and looked down at the pilots gathered around. The room grew quiet. Lady Ginette met Sharon's gaze.

"There are six deliveries waiting," Sharon said.

"Just catching our breath, Flight Captain." Ginette smiled.

Sharon caught the condescending tone attached to the words "Flight Captain." "While you lot are catching your breath, aircraft aren't being delivered." She passed out the chits. "Now get to the duty Anson and get moving!"

The pilots, led by Lady Ginette, gathered their kit and headed out of the door.

Sharon saw that Mother did not smile at any of them. He met Sharon's gaze. Not a word passed between them. She went to pour herself a cup of coffee. Her hands shook as she added cream and sugar.

CHAPTER 20
[WEDNESDAY, DECEMBER 6, 1944]

Sharon had a few minutes to think as she sat in the back seat of the Anson while it flew the short distance to the Hawker factory's Langley Airfield on the south side of London. *This is the first trip into Holland. It's only a short hop to Volkel in a Tempest. Less than an hour.* As she did before every flight, she'd calculated time, course, and distance in her mind. Still, she wasn't prepared for the reality she saw upon reaching Holland. From the air, Volkel was the typical stretch of runways in the shape of an awkward X. Bomb craters concentrated at the centre of the X and spread out across the surrounding snow-coated farmland.

Sharon landed on the repaired runway and taxied to a hangar, which was more rubble than building. She shut down the massive Napier engine and watched the propeller slow to a stop. She went through her final checks, climbed out of the cockpit, and slid down the wing into a pile of snow.

A mechanic, bundled in so many layers of clothing he was almost unrecognizable, looked her over. "NAFFI wagon is there." He hitched a thumb over his right shoulder.

Sharon stamped the snow from her boots, took her parachute in one hand and her kit bag in another. She looked at a gathering of tents.

About fifty yards from the canvas encampment were the remains of several wrecked aircraft. Some were Allied and others bore swastikas.

In five minutes, she had a cup of coffee and a sandwich and was sitting at a table inside a tent with its familiar scent: a mixture of green-dyed canvas, sweat, coffee, and greasy food.

An RAF pilot at the next table said, "Christ, first we bomb the hell out of Volkel, then we fix it up enough to fly out of it so we can live in tents. Ain't war grand?"

A New Zealand pilot said, "At least the grub is tolerable."

The third pilot was from Canada. "Intolerable."

The sound of a circling aircraft reached their ears, then the siren of a crash wagon headed for the runway.

"Something's up!" The three pilots got up and went outside. Sharon stuffed the remainder of the sandwich in her mouth, picked up her coffee, and followed.

The three pilots looked up. Sharon did the same and saw a Tempest circling. One leg of the plane's landing gear was down; the other remained stubbornly tucked in its wing.

"He'd better bail out." The Canadian pointed to the pile of wrecked aircraft. "Remember what happened to Freddy when he tried a wheels-up landing?"

The New Zealander nodded.

"Burnt right down to the bone," the RAF pilot said.

They watched as the pilot climbed to about eight thousand feet. He rolled the Tempest on its back. The pilot dropped out. Sharon waited for the parachute to open.

The chute blossomed. The wind caught the silk and the pilot drifted north.

Sharon remembered to breathe.

The pilotless Tempest started an inverted flat spin and hit the ground about half a mile away. The sound of the explosion from the resultant fireball reached them seconds later.

A Jeep started up. They watched it drive after the pilot, who grew smaller as the wind carried him north.

Half an hour later, Douglas arrived in the Anson. He squeezed out the back door, waved at Sharon, and headed for the latrine. Ten minutes after taking on fuel and refills of coffee, they walked toward the Anson.

A Jeep pulled up. The top was down despite the winter cold. In the back of the Jeep, a body was wrapped in a parachute. The three pilots came out of the tent.

"What happened?" the New Zealander asked.

"The wind carried the poor bastard to the river," said the Jeep driver. "He drowned."

Douglas took Sharon by the elbow and insisted she climb inside first. He brushed past her into the cockpit. It took ten minutes for them to get off of the ground. When they leveled out at five thousand feet, he pointed north. "Jerry has blown the dykes. Looks like the winter will get worse for the poor bastards behind the German lines. The Nazis cut off food supplies because the Dutch helped the Allies at Market Garden. With the flooding and so little food, I'm afraid a lot of people will starve before spring."

Sharon thought, *I just want to go home. Europe can fight its fucking wars without me.*

Douglas flew west. Sharon looked out the window and saw the edge of what appeared to be a massive lake stretching as far as the eye could see. She longed to see the Rocky Mountains on the western horizon.

CHAPTER 21
[FRIDAY, DECEMBER 15, 1944]

"Here's a letter from Honeysuckle. She and Sean are travelling south to spend Christmas with us." Linda handed the letter to Sharon, who sat in the wing-backed chair in the front room of the cottage.

"What about Michael?" Sharon asked.

"We'd better let him know. Has he been very busy at Bletchley Park?" Linda sat down across from Sharon.

"He says they have the commandos guarding the grounds. He's beginning to wonder if the commandos are there to keep him from escaping. Will you invite Milton?" Sharon asked.

Linda looked at her feet. "He's been transferred to the continent."

Sharon looked at her friend. *The fighting is nasty there and the casualties are high. I hope he makes it back.*

Linda raised her head and looked through tears at Sharon. "Do you think he'll make it home safe?"

CHAPTER 22

[SUNDAY, DECEMBER 17, 1944]

"According to Robert, Jerry is counterattacking through the Ardennes." Mother sat across the table from Sharon, leaning on his elbows.

"And I'm hearing the weather has closed in. Heavy snow is falling, and we can't fly." Sharon looked at the mixture of coffee, cream, and sugar at the bottom of her cup.

"You'd think we'd learn. The Nazis invaded France through the Ardennes in 1940. It feels like we're back at square one with this war." Mother lifted his cup and drained the remains of his tea.

They sat alone in the canteen. Sharon had ordered all pilots to get some rest. She'd stayed to handle any priority deliveries. "Hitler's Army isn't what it once was."

"But he has Me 262 jet fighters and V-2 rockets. We don't have anything like the V-2." Mother's eyes shifted nervously from his cup to the pot set at the centre of the table.

Sharon caught a nod from the cook. She got up and walked to the kitchen. "Thank you." She returned with two plates of bacon and eggs.

Mother picked up a knife and fork. Then he got up and refilled Sharon's coffee. Sharon folded a piece of bread around two slices of bacon and dipped it into her egg yolk. She chewed and thought.

"Remember Edgar?" she asked.

Mother used his hand to cover a mouth full of egg as he looked up at her. "Rather hard to forget."

Sharon took another bite of bacon and bread. "He taught me to look for evidence. To use what I actually saw with my own eyes to reach conclusions about what was really happening in this war instead of listening to what I was being told was going on."

Mother chewed, poured more tea, and waited.

"We're eating bacon and eggs," Sharon continued. "Food supplies are getting through. That was not the case in '40, '41, and '42. I've seen what our bombs have done to the U-boat pens along the coast. It looks like Hitler is running out of ports to launch his submarines." Sharon tucked the rest of her bacon sandwich into her mouth.

"What about Hitler's new weapons?" Mother asked.

He's enjoying this back-and-forth. Sharon reached for her coffee and sipped. She put the cup down and wrapped some bacon in another slice of bread. "He's running out of places to launch them. Yes, they're terrible weapons, and yes, Harry was killed by one. But you haven't seen the number of fighters, bombers, and transport aircraft I've seen. The airfields are jammed with them. And you haven't seen the way the ports here and on the continent are filled with ships unloading all manner of equipment."

Mother took a sip of tea.

"Besides, if the BBC is to be believed, Hitler is almost entirely surrounded. He's got us to the west and south. The Russians are invading from the east, and the Nazis have retreated behind Germany's borders. It's only a matter of time now." Sharon dabbed her bread and bacon in another yolk.

"You're saying I'm being an alarmist for worrying about this attack, then?" Mother used his fork and knife to cut a slice of bacon in half.

Sharon looked at her sandwich before putting it in her mouth. "I'm saying that nowadays, I'm more worried about the likes of my Uncle Marmaduke, Lady Ginette, and Edwin Beck." She took a bite of her sandwich.

Mother frowned. "Beck is the kind of man who loves war, but the other two, they're British."

"Lady Ginette and Marmaduke were members of the British Union of Fascists before the war. I have the documents to prove it. And I also have the documents to show that my Uncle Marmaduke has made a fortune through his investments in steel, munitions, and textiles. All from the safety of West Yorkshire." Sharon waited for Mother's reaction.

"A war profiteer?" Mother asked.

"All of it strictly legal." Sharon reached for her coffee.

"I see."

Sharon could feel the anger rising up off the man like the steam from his cup of tea. His face, however, remained impassive. She said, "They are the ones we will have to fight after this war is over. It will be a different kind of war, but it will be a war."

"You're certain of this?"

Sharon nodded as she lifted her coffee cup and held it in both hands. "I am. All I need to do is look at the evidence. Marmaduke and Lady Ginette want a return to the class system where they have money, status, and power. Beck wants a class system where the colour of his skin gives him power over other people. After the war, people like you and me — people who fought in this war — will have other battles to fight. It might be more like a civil war, but it will be a war nonetheless."

"You learned this from Edgar?"

"He taught me to pay attention to what was going on around us." Sharon pointed to the door. "And it all happens just outside that door." She pointed at the empty table where Ginette always held court. "Or right over there."

Mother nodded. "My friend Robert has been saying much the same thing."

How come I get the feeling that Robert is more than a friend to you, Mother?

CHAPTER 23

[SATURDAY, DECEMBER 23, 1944]

Sharon woke up as the wheels of the Anson touched the runway. *Where the hell am I?* She looked out the window to see the familiar outline of the White Waltham hangar. The low sun lengthened the shadows and painted an orange hue along the edges of the buildings. *The days will be getting longer now.* She smiled.

She looked forward and saw Douglas at the controls. He taxied the Anson to the apron in front of the hangar and shut down the engines. Sharon was the last pilot out, and she savoured the fresh silence.

Douglas stepped out of the side door and onto the grass, then turned to her. "How many deliveries today?"

"Five. Mostly Typhoons. With the weather clearing, they're pounding the Nazi tanks and supply lines in Belgium."

"You must be knackered." Douglas released his parachute harness, stretched, and dropped his chin.

Sharon smiled at Douglas's impression of exhaustion. "I am that."

Douglas looked outside of the aircraft. "What's got her wind up?"

Sharon nodded at the hangar. Lady Ginette looked like an overripe pear in her white flight suit. She was waving her arms about as she faced Ernie and Walter. Sharon closed the distance and stepped onto the concrete apron in front of the hangar.

"I told you! I don't want him," she pointed at Ernie, "working on my aircraft!"

Sharon stepped up behind Lady Ginette and caught an overpowering whiff of Chanel perfume. *Where do you get Chanel in the middle of a war?*

Lady Ginette turned on Walter. Her voice shook with emotion. "You and your kind need to know your place."

"What place is that?" Sharon sensed rather than saw a gathering of people around the mouth of the hangar.

Lady Ginette turned. Sharon saw the woman's face was red with anger. But it was the rage behind her eyes that struck her most. *She's revealing the ugliness behind her polite façade.*

"I don't want that jigaboo working on my aircraft." Lady Ginette shook her finger in the air.

Sharon felt the calm focus of pre-combat clarity. "Why, Lady Ginette, your fascist leanings are showing."

"What?" Lady Ginette stepped back, startled.

You started this, Ginette, and I'm going to finish it. Sharon slowed her words so they would carry to everyone within earshot. "You were a member of the British Union of Fascists."

"How could you know that?" Lady Ginette asked.

Sharon shrugged. She felt the massive presence of Douglas at her side. "Ernie and Walter joined up to fight the Nazis. You wanted to join the Nazis."

Lady Ginette looked around her, rolled her eyes, puffed out her chest, and retreated in the direction of the dispersal hut. "I've had enough of mongrels and colonials."

Sharon moved closer to Ernie and Walter. "What else has been happening around here today?"

Ernie looked at Walter. Walter took off his green wool cap, rubbed the top of his head, pulled the cap back on, and with an exaggerated back-country accent said, "Been running like a couple of hens being chased 'round the yard by a mangy coot of a dog."

"I could sure use a cup of coffee. How about the pair of you?" Sharon asked.

Walter turned and pointed himself in the direction of the canteen.

"Where are you going?" Sharon asked.

"To get some coffee for us," he said.

"Like hell you are." Ernie put his hand on Walter's shoulder. "How many coffees?" He looked at Douglas.

"Four, please." Sharon looked around her for confirmation.

Douglas nodded. "I'll give you a hand." He followed Ernie to the canteen.

"We'll need somewhere to sit." Sharon set her parachute on a nearby shelf and arranged crates and upturned buckets for them to sit on. Wordlessly, Walter did the same until they had a circle of makeshift seats.

Ernie and Douglas returned with coffee cups, sugar, and milk. "Mother sent this along," Ernie said, pulling a bottle of rum from the pocket of his coveralls.

After they sat down with their doctored coffees, Walter turned to Sharon. "You were in Belgium today?"

"And Holland and France." Sharon savoured the magical mixture of rum and coffee. Her toes began to tingle with warmth.

"What are you hearing about Hitler's offensive?" Walter asked.

"Not much. The talk was more about finding ways to hit back after the weather finally cleared. You heard about Malmady?" Sharon inhaled the alcoholic fumes from her coffee and coughed. *I put too much rum in there.*

Ernie used his cup to point at Walter. "We're hearing the SS murdered about eighty American POWs there."

Douglas nodded. "I heard that happened on the seventeenth. The story spread along the line, and instead of retreating, the soldiers started to fight."

Sharon looked up as two more pilots arrived with their coffee cups. "Mind if we join you?"

Walter stood up.

"Pull up a seat." Sharon pointed at a crate.

The two young women perched side by side on the upturned wooden crate. Ernie hefted the bottle of rum. "Help yourselves."

Linda walked into the hangar. "Is everyone invited?"

Sharon said, "Of course."

Linda pulled up a pail, turned it upside down, and sat next to her sister-in-law.

"The weather just began to clear," Sharon said, "so the Typhoons and Thunderbolts have been ordered to hammer the Panzers and Jerry's supply lines." She looked over her shoulder. News of the hangar gathering had spread. Other pilots arrived and perched on whatever was available.

Mother arrived with a tray of cups and a pot of coffee. He set them down, then pulled a bottle of rum out of each of his jacket pockets. He held the bottles up. "Would anyone like more coffee?"

Sharon said, "Join us!"

He leaned against the fuselage of an Anson and smiled. "I'll stick with tea, if you don't mind."

"Exactly what kind of tea are you drinking?" Linda asked.

"Fortified." Mother raised his cup. "Cheers."

Ernie raised his cup. "To Edgar!"

There was quiet. Ernie looked embarrassed. Walter had tears in his eyes.

"To Molly Hume!" One of the young women raised her glass.

The room grew quieter still.

Sharon raised her glass, took a drink, then let the silence stretch out before turning to Walter. "What are you hearing about the goings-on in the Ardennes?"

"Patton is on the move, Monty is holding back, and guys like me are looking for a fight." Walter glanced at Ernie.

Ernie said, "Eleven black POWs from the 333rd were tortured and murdered by the SS in Wereth, Belgium. Same day as those boys in Malmady." Ernie nodded at Walter.

"Not as many people know about it, but the news got the guys in the 761st Tank Battalion pretty motivated." Walter looked around at the faces of the people who were intent on what he was saying. "The 761st are called the Black Panthers. They're with General Patton."

"Now that the weather is clearing, we're going to be busy replacing the losses from all of this fighting," Sharon said.

"So we won't be home for Christmas?" Linda had a smile on her face.

Douglas laughed and raised his cup. "Again!"

Walter smiled. "When Edgar and me were ten, it was Christmas, and we'd saved up enough to buy a cigar at the corner store. Somehow, his mother heard about it, and she found us around back just as we were lighting up. Edgar's mom was a tiny woman. She had to stand on her toes to grab him by the ear. I can still see him leaning toward her with her hanging onto his ear and him askin' her to let go."

This started a series of funny Christmas stories that had everyone laughing.

Mother walked over to Sharon and leaned close to her right ear. "Lady Ginette has left. She spent a very theatrical thirty minutes in the dispersal hut, telling everyone who would listen about how she was wronged and falsely accused of being a Nazi sympathizer. When I left, there were only two people left to listen to her. The rest came here to join the party."

Sharon turned to him. "Do we have another duty pilot available to replace her and fly the Anson?"

Mother nodded.

"Good." Sharon looked around at the smiling gathering. *Enjoy this. It won't last very long.*

Ten minutes later, a Jeep pulled up in front of the hangar. Sergeant Beck stepped out and came inside.

"What the hell is he doing here?" Ernie asked.

Beck pointed a white-gloved finger at Walter. "Time to go, Coleman."

Walter stood up and followed the sergeant back to the Jeep. Sharon stepped outside and watched as Walter clambered into the back seat. She looked around and saw that all of the people who had been inside the hangar were now outside waving to Walter.

Beck frowned.

Sharon turned and saw Ernie standing back. Despite the rum's effects, she recognized the undisguised hatred in Ernie's eyes.

CHAPTER 24
[MONDAY, DECEMBER 25, 1944]

"Phone call for you." Mother held the phone's heavy black receiver in the air and pointed it at Sharon. She stopped eating her breakfast, stood up, and walked to the phone. Mother held his hand over the receiver. "Colonel McBride."

Sharon swallowed. "Lacey here."

"This is Colonel McBride. I'm Airman Coleman's commanding officer."

Sharon heard a southern United States accent. "What happened to Colonel Wilson?"

"Transferred to the continent. Unfortunately, he was reported killed in action two days ago. But that's not why I'm calling."

Sharon waited. There was something in McBride's tone that made her wary.

"Yesterday evening, Sergeant Beck was in a traffic accident."

"And?" Sharon looked out the window at the side of the White Waltham hangar.

"He was killed in the accident."

Sharon closed her eyes and recalled the look she'd seen in Ernie's eyes when Beck picked up Walter on Saturday evening. "Did you know Beck?"

"No. But I do have some questions I would like to ask. Colonel Wilson left extensive notes about you, Airman Coleman, and an Airman Washington. Washington is deceased?"

"Murdered, actually," Sharon said.

"According to Colonel Wilson's notes, he was told to stop fighting and did not."

"I was there. Edgar Washington was unarmed, moved to protect me from a drunken paratrooper, and was shot in cold blood by Sergeant Beck." Sharon had a flashback of the life vacating Edgar's eyes.

"That is why I would like to speak with you in person. There are several inconsistencies I was hoping you might clear up."

"When?" Sharon asked.

"Tomorrow?"

"With the German offensive and Allied counterattacks, I'm afraid we are stretched very thin. Would you be able to come here tomorrow morning before dawn?" Sharon looked at Mother. He nodded.

"Say zero six hundred?" McBride asked.

"We'll meet over breakfast." Sharon hung up and held the phone out. Mother took it. "Wilson's replacement?"

Sharon nodded. *What is McBride after?*

At dusk, she could smell supper as she opened the front door of the cottage. It was a medley of ham, potatoes, carrots, and peas. Her mouth began to water.

Sean stood up from his chair. "We were beginning to think you might not make it." He handed her a package wrapped in red paper.

Sharon took the package and caressed the crepe paper with her fingertips. "What's this?"

Linda and Honeysuckle stepped into the room. An atmosphere of expectation permeated the air.

Sharon unwrapped the package. She found a black wooden box and opened it.

Honeysuckle said, "The earrings are from us. The ring is from Cornelia."

Sharon saw the gold earrings with white pearl insets. The ring was also made of gold with a sparkling red ruby. "How?"

"Michael found the earrings," Honeysuckle said. "Cornelia, your niece, brought the ring over. She told us that her father was away on business. And she said that your grandmother wanted you to have that ring. I was very impressed by your niece, by the way."

Sharon changed out her earrings and slipped the ring on next to her wedding band. The ring fit perfectly. "Thank you." She felt the warm presence of her mother.

"Can we eat now?" Sean asked.

They moved into the kitchen and crammed around a table where bowls and plates competed for space. Sharon savoured the vegetables and ham Honeysuckle had brought with her. She glanced at her fifteen-year-old brother, who was tucking away food at an astonishing rate. Sharon looked at Honeysuckle, who was watching Sean eat. Then Sharon looked at Linda. *This is the first Christmas without Harry. Michael couldn't get away from Bletchley Park because of the Battle of the Bulge, and Milton is somewhere in France or Holland. Maybe we'll all be together next Christmas.*

CHAPTER 25

[TUESDAY, DECEMBER 26, 1944]

Sharon gathered her hair at the back, held it there with a rubber band, then flipped it back over her shoulder. She felt and found a gritty bit of sleep in the corner of her right eye, and removed it with the nail of her pinky finger. She sipped from her second cup of coffee and looked out the window of the White Waltham dispersal hut.

A grey Buick stopped on a patch of gravel. The car had white stars on the front door and hood. A man stepped out of the driver's door, looked around, saw Sharon watching him through the window, and walked toward her. He opened the door and took off his cap. He looked to be in his late forties. He had grey hair on the sides, and thinning hair on top. He was a bit taller than her and broad across the shoulders. He opened the door and stepped inside.

"Flight Captain Lacey?"

Sharon nodded. His uniform was clean, his tan pants pressed, and his brown uniform jacket buttoned up. He bore himself with practiced dignity. He offered his hand, and she shook it. He said, "Colonel McBride. Thank you for meeting me during such a busy time."

"Coffee?" Sharon asked.

"Yes, please."

Sharon pointed to the coffee urn and cups. "Help yourself."

"Of course." The colonel walked over and poured himself a cup.

"Bacon and eggs okay?" Sharon sat down at a table. She lifted her chin as a signal to the cook who waited at the door and disappeared into the kitchen.

"Of course. Eggs sunny side up, please." Colonel McBride turned and saw that Sharon had sat down. He sat down across from her. Sharon waited as he settled himself in and checked that his tie was knotted neatly at his throat.

"Where would you like to start?" he asked.

"Where are you from?" Sharon studied the man's reaction. He looked a bit surprised by the question. His grey eyes studied her for at least ten seconds.

"Richmond, Virginia. How about you?"

Sharon smiled. "Calgary, Alberta."

"Where's that?"

"You know where Montana is?"

McBride nodded.

"North of there." Sharon looked right and saw the cook open the kitchen door. She got up and was handed two plates. She returned to the table and set a plate down in front of McBride and the other at her spot.

"Want a refill?" McBride lifted his cup.

"Yes, please." *I wonder how long the civility will last?*

"I have a daughter your age." McBride sat back down with the coffees, then used his fork to cut into one egg.

Sharon folded a piece of bacon inside a slice of bread.

"She's a nurse like her mother." McBride lifted a forkful of egg to his mouth.

Sharon put her elbows on the table and looked at him. "Are you patronizing me?"

McBride had a mouthful of egg. He frowned at the disadvantageous spot she'd maneuvered him into.

"You know what I mean," Sharon continued. "Women shouldn't be in the Air Force. It's not the *right* kind of feminine pursuit." She studied his facial features and the smile that appeared in his eyes.

McBride chewed and covered his mouth. "My other daughter is a WASP — a Women's Air Service Pilot."

I really put my foot in it this time. "Where is she flying?"

"Back home. She loves to fly. That's probably how I ended up here. I had to learn to fly so that she could." He lifted his cup to sip some coffee. "I'm actually a lawyer by trade. I'm here to gather some facts. You see, there are a variety of opinions about Sergeant Beck. His supporters say he was simply a patriot doing his job as a military policeman. There are others who say he was a racist and a murderer. I suspect by your previous comments about Washington that you will fall into the latter category. I also thought that you might be able to shed some light on his character. You are, after all, a Canadian with a slightly different point of view." McBride picked up a piece of bacon and popped it into his mouth. The smile continued to light his eyes.

"Beck treated Edgar like he was subhuman. He shot Edgar for no other reason than that he was black." Sharon sat back and cradled her coffee in her hands. *How will you react to that?*

"You know this for a certainty?"

"I watched the Sergeant's behaviour over several months. And I witnessed the murder. Edgar was only a few feet away from me when he was shot. I heard what was said. I saw what happened." Sharon lifted her cup to her lips.

"There is a complication you may not be aware of." McBride looked at his plate and picked up another piece of bacon. "The maintenance chief at the motor pool took a look at the wreck of the Jeep Beck was driving. He found that the brake seals had deteriorated. He checked the brake fluid reservoir and found that it had been contaminated with motor oil."

"I don't understand." In another part of Sharon's mind, a memory began to swim its way to the surface. *Maybe you do understand.*

"Either a mistake was made and oil was added instead of brake fluid. Or someone intentionally sabotaged the sergeant's Jeep." McBride picked up his fork. "I've been told that motor oil eats away at the rubber seals of the brake cylinders and that's what caused the brake failure leading to the sergeant's death."

"You're telling me you think he was murdered?" Sharon asked.

"No, at least not yet. As I said, I'm just gathering facts." McBride popped bacon into his mouth.

Sharon felt her anger rising. "So a white MP dies in what may or may not have been an accident, and you are here to investigate. Yet when an unarmed black man is shot and killed in front of me, I'm told that there is a war on and no action will be taken against the murderer."

McBride chewed his food and watched her.

This guy is no pushover. Now's the time to find out what he's made of. "Did you hear about what happened at Malmady?" Sharon asked.

"Over eighty American prisoners of war were executed by the SS." He continued to study her.

Sharon picked up the coffee cup and pointed with her index finger. "Did you hear about what happened near Wereth, Belgium on the same day?"

McBride covered his mouth. "No, I did not."

"It's a fact that you need to become familiar with. Come and talk with me after you find out." Sharon stood up and picked up her kit. "I've got a priority delivery."

She left Colonel McBride to finish his breakfast alone.

CHAPTER 26
[MONDAY, JANUARY 1, 1945]

"Hello, Sharon." Michael sat in a chair at the cottage. Yellow light filtered its way through the lampshade to cast shadows across the floral patterns on the wall. "I thought we might go out for supper."

Sharon dropped her shoulder bag and embraced her husband. She breathed in the familiar scent of dusty tobacco and wool. She found herself crying.

"I didn't mean to upset you. Linda phoned me and told me that I'd missed Christmas, and I'd better not miss New Year's. She said she'd be away tonight. That she was meeting Milton in Paris." Michael wiped away Sharon's tears with his thumb.

"Linda phoned you?" Sharon lifted her head to look at Michael. She saw that he'd cut his blond hair short. It made his blue eyes seem bigger.

Michael nodded. "Well, are we going out for dinner?"

"When do you have to head back?"

"Tomorrow morning." He combed his fingers through her hair.

"Can't we just stay here?" Sharon tucked the side of her face against his chest.

"That would be fine."

CHAPTER 27
[TUESDAY, JANUARY 2, 1945]

Sharon closed and locked the front door of the cottage,
then waved as Michael drove away in a black saloon car. When the car
was out of sight, she turned and walked in the other direction toward
White Waltham. *Why didn't you tell him?*

She looked down the lane where it curved between a pair of rock
walls. The rising sun was just over the horizon, making it possible for
her to see where she was headed. *Because I know, but I don't know
how to explain that I know.*

She reached the curve in the lane, turned left through a gate, and
walked across an open field of grass that reached half way to her knees.
The grass was damp and she was glad she wore her flying boots. *Besides,
if anyone else finds out, I'll be grounded.*

She reached the stone wall at the end of the field, walked though
another gate, and followed the road to the airfield. She heard the sound
of an aircraft engine. *Ernie's warming up the Anson.* She felt gravel
under her feet and pulled the collar of her Irvin jacket up to keep her
ears and neck warm.

*My mother knew right away. She told me one time when I asked about
her and my father. When I asked her how she knew, she shrugged and
said, "I just did."* Sharon turned when she heard a vehicle approaching.

It was a Jeep. She looked closer and saw that Walter was driving. He pulled up alongside and opened the canvas door. "You want a ride the rest of the way?"

"Thanks." Sharon climbed in and closed the door. Walter released the clutch, and the Jeep rolled forward. "I thought an MP had to drive you."

Walter shifted into third. "McBride called me in yesterday. Said that he checked my file and saw that I was a driver. He asked if I was fine with driving myself to the base every morning."

"What do you think of him?"

Walter shifted into fourth. "He salutes me just the same as he does anyone else. Colonel Wilson never did." Walter downshifted, braked, and turned into the roadway leading to White Waltham. He stopped in front of the dispersal hut. "Okay if I park here, boss?"

Sharon turned and caught his smile. "Oh, I suppose."

Inside the hut, Mother stopped them with a raised hand. "There's been a major attack on our airfields in Holland, Belgium, and northern France. The call is out for replacements. We're looking at a big push over the next few days."

Sharon approached Brussels Evere Airfield. On finals, she saw a row of burned-out B-17 Flying Fortresses. After landing, she taxied over rumbling steel matting. Either side of the taxiway was piled with snow dotted with the charred corpses of Typhoons and Spitfires destroyed by the Luftwaffe attack of the day before. She maneuvered her Spitfire by zigzagging because her forward vision was blocked by the fighter's long nose. She stopped in front of a hangar that was peppered with holes. She shut down, released her harness, opened the cockpit door, and stepped out onto the wing.

Once on the ground, she looked around and saw two members of the ground crew approaching. "We're glad to get this one." The taller of the pair had a French Canadian accent.

"How many aircraft did you lose yesterday?" Sharon asked.

"The press is saying it was a victory for us," said the taller one.

The shorter man laughed. "Frenchy's pulling your leg. We lost more than a hundred aircraft destroyed on the ground. I don't know how that can be counted as a victory."

Sharon heard the oddly flavoured Irish accent in the shorter man's voice. *He must be from Newfoundland.*

"Newfie counted a hundred wrecks, then stopped. After that, there wasn't much point," Frenchy said.

"Are any still flying?" Sharon asked.

"A handful." Newfie pointed at the Spitfire Sharon delivered. "That'll make up for the one we lost this morning."

The pair began to push the Spitfire into the hangar. Sharon took one wing, while Frenchy took the tail and Newfie the other wing. They swung the fighter around so that its nose pointed out the hangar door.

"Merci." Frenchy slid under the wing to begin the process of checking the cannons.

Newfie went under the opposite wing.

Sharon hefted her kit and made for the canteen. It was filled with pilots. Some were asleep in their chairs. Others talked quietly at tables. The mood was somber. Sharon grabbed a cup of coffee, doctored it with cream and sugar, drank it, and felt the warmth reaching her fingers. She filled her cup a second time.

A clutch of five pilots sat at a table near the urn.

"Anybody see what happened to Cardinal?" an RAF pilot asked.

"No," said a pilot with a South African accent.

Sharon felt a shiver run through her. "Cardinal? Milton Cardinal?"

The pilots turned to look at Sharon. The RAF pilot wore an Irvine Jacket. He asked, "You know him?"

Sharon nodded.

"Four of us did a trip to the German airbase at Wiesbaden. We got into a scrap with some Focke-Wulfs. None of us saw what happened to Cardinal." He took Sharon's coffee cup from her.

Sharon looked down and stared at her empty right hand as if it belonged to someone else. She stared at the coffee she'd spilled over her flying boots and the wooden floor.

Linda opened the front door of the cottage. "Sharon?"

Sharon sat in the kitchen with a cold cup of coffee. She looked up at Linda as she stepped into the kitchen. She tried to talk, but began to cry instead.

"What happened?" Linda sat down across from Sharon. "Something's happened to Michael?" She shucked her way out of her Irvine jacket.

Sharon shook her head.

"Sean? My mother?" She hung the sheepskin jacket on the back of the chair.

Sharon shook her head.

"Oh no! It's Milton, isn't it? Something happened to Milton?"

Sharon nodded. "Missing."

Linda sat back in her chair. "How do you know?"

Sharon looked at her hands. "I was at Evere. Some pilots were talking about Cardinal not returning from a morning patrol."

Linda looked at the ceiling. "I just saw him in Paris. You wouldn't believe what it's like there. That city is coming back to life. It's wonderful."

"They said that no one saw what happened to him."

Linda wiped her eyes. "We were in Paris for a day. We had so much fun." Linda looked at her friend. "Are you sure it was him?"

Sharon shrugged. *What can I say?*

Linda shook her head. "Shit. Shit. Shit!"

Forty-five minutes later, the phone rang and Sharon answered.

"I took a break from reading the mail," said Michael's voice, "and I saw Milton's name on the casualty list. Have you heard anything?"

CHAPTER 28
[FRIDAY, JANUARY 12, 1945]

The phone at White Waltham rang. Mother held it out for Sharon. He looked past her at Linda, who was staring at nothing in particular.

Sharon took the phone. "Lacey."

Colonel McBride said, "You asked me to find out what happened in Wereth, Belgium. Eleven men were tortured and killed by the SS. They were Americans from the 333rd who were prisoners of war."

"And?" Sharon asked.

"The men were black."

"Then why do we hear about Malmady and not about Wereth?" Sharon looked out the window and wished she could see Edgar one more time.

"You think that Edgar's death was the result of bigotry, and that same bigotry is the reason why we don't hear about the murders in Wereth."

Sharon noted that McBride had not asked a question, but made a statement.

"I did what you asked."

Sharon waited a moment before replying. "Yes. I'll give you credit for that."

"And I am calling about something completely different. I need a favour."

I was ready for almost everything but this.

"You must know that we have had heavy casualties after Hitler's offensive in the Ardennes."

"Yes, I've seen some of the damage done." Sharon looked over at Linda. *And I'm looking at some of it now.*

"We fly our wounded back to the States. Because of the Luftwaffe attacks on the Allied airfields in Holland and Belgium, there is a shortage of transport aircraft and crews to fly them." McBride took a breath.

"What did you have in mind?" Sharon tried to think ahead.

"Could you supply a crew for a C-54? You'd need a pilot, co-pilot, and an engineer. The crew needs to leave now, pick up the aircraft at Croydon, then fly it to Prestwick. I've had to call in a few favours to get the aircraft."

"Whose aircraft is it?" Sharon asked.

"You don't want to know. Do you have a crew?"

"Yes. You will need to free up Airman Coleman."

"Is he a qualified flight engineer?" McBride asked.

"Do you want a crew or don't you?"

"Coleman is yours."

"Have the aircraft ready. We're leaving now. Will you meet us there?" Sharon hung up the phone before he could answer.

We've almost caught up on deliveries after the New Year's Day attacks on the continental airfields. Mother can run things. Sharon walked toward Linda, who turned to her sister-in-law with weary eyes.

"I've got a delivery to make at Prestwick," Sharon said. "It leaves right away. It would be better with two pilots. It's a C-54." As Linda thought it over, Sharon turned to Mother. "We have a flight to Prestwick. Can you keep an eye on things until we get back?"

Mother smiled. "I always do. Have a grand time in Scotland, lassies. Douglas will be out in a minute." He pointed in the direction of the toilet. Then Mother nodded at Sharon. His eyes looked over her shoulder.

Sharon turned. Linda had her kit in hand and was walking toward her friend. "Well? Are you ready to go or aren't you?"

They stepped out the door and made their way down to the hangar.

Ernie and Walter were staring at the engine of a De Havilland Rapide. Ernie said, "I think we need to swap the magneto out."

"Can you handle things on your own for a day or two?" Sharon asked Ernie.

"What's up?" Ernie asked.

"We need Walter for a trip in a C-54." Sharon looked over her shoulder as Douglas walked past on his way to the Anson.

"Come on, ladies, this war waits for neither man nor woman. And I'm a stone lighter for this trip to Croydon." Douglas gave them a rakish wink.

Ernie looked at Walter. "Where are you going?" Walter asked.

"Croydon, then Prestwick. I told McBride you would be our flight engineer." Sharon looked over her shoulder as Linda followed Douglas. He walked around the Anson doing the preflight check.

"Where the hell is Prestwick?" Walter began wiping his hands on a cloth.

"Northern Scotland. Are you coming?" Sharon asked.

"Put on a fresh pair of coveralls. I'll grab you a parachute," Ernie said.

In less than half an hour, they climbed out of the Anson and stood looking up at the nose of a silver four-engine C-54 with *Sunflower II* painted on its nose.

Linda tapped Sharon on the shoulder. "I'll do the walkaround while you get ready for takeoff." Linda turned to Walter. "Would you?" She handed him her parachute and bag.

Walter followed Sharon up the steps. The cavernous interior of the aircraft was already modified to support stretchers. A framework of litter supports was attached to either side of the fuselage.

Sharon turned and walked toward the cockpit. She stowed her parachute, then eased herself into the pilot's chair. Walter stashed two more parachutes and Linda's bag, then looked over Sharon's shoulder as she took the checklist from the dash and began to read.

"You ever flown one of these before?" Walter asked.

Sharon shook her head. "First time."

Walter looked at the gauges in front of Sharon and above her head.

He turned, stepped out of the cockpit, turned, walked along the interior, and went down the steps. He saw Linda peering up into the nose of the aircraft. "Sharon's never flown one of these before," he said.

"That's right." Linda looked over her shoulder at Walter and saw the worry on his face. "This is what we do, Walter. This is what we've been trained to do. We fly all sorts of aircraft. Sharon is very good at it. That's why I'm doing the exterior check while she familiarizes herself with the controls. This trip means we work as a team."

"Why am I here?" Walter looked down along the belly of the aircraft.

"We need another set of eyes. Four engines mean more instruments to monitor. McBride wanted a crew of three, so we're it." Linda inspected the undercarriage leg of the nose wheel.

Walter leaned down and looked past Linda. "Here he comes."

Linda stood up and looked right. McBride's Buick pulled up. The colonel stepped out of the car.

Walter stood away from Linda and saluted the colonel. McBride returned the courtesy, then asked, "How soon will you be in the air?"

Linda looked at her watch, stepped away from the nose, and looked up. Sharon saw them through the side window and waved. A minute later, she was standing alongside them under the nose.

Linda looked at Sharon. "The colonel wants to know how soon we can leave."

Sharon thought for a moment. "We need to complete our checks. Say half an hour?"

"Sir?"

They turned and saw McBride's driver, a man who looked too young to shave. He stood just inside the open door at the base of the control tower. "Call for you, sir," the driver said.

"Excuse me for a moment." McBride walked to the tower then inside.

"Walter, are you worried about us flying this machine?" Linda asked.

Walter looked at each of them and shook his head no. "What's my job?"

"Another pair of eyes. Another pair of hands," Sharon said. "Once we're in the air, we'll show you what you need to do. You okay with that?"

McBride strode toward them. "There's been a change in plans."

"What's up?" Sharon waited for him to come closer.

"A mechanical problem in Belgium. We need you to fly there, pick up the wounded men, and fly them to Prestwick." McBride crossed his arms and stood with his feet shoulder-width apart.

"Says who?" Sharon asked.

Walter took a breath.

"It's been cleared by d'Erlanger." McBride's voice had the added edge of command.

Sharon looked at Linda and Walter. "You two okay with that?"

Linda shrugged. "Those boys need a ride home."

Walter asked, "Home?"

"I'm assuming that when we refuel at Prestwick, we'll be told there are no extra crews and we'll be ordered on to Greenland, Newfoundland, and. . ." Sharon looked at McBride, then smiled.

McBride blushed. His arms dropped. "The wounded are amputees. They need to get to McGuire General Hospital in Richmond, Virginia."

"Why not tell us that from the beginning?" Sharon studied the colonel's face and watched his defenses fall.

"We didn't exactly get off to a good start. And. . ." McBride began. The three waited. ". . .I'm tired of all the killing. I'd like to get those boys home. Do something I can be proud of."

"Why didn't you say that in the first place?" Sharon looked at Linda and Walter. "Okay with you two?"

Walter nodded. Linda did the same.

Sharon looked at McBride. *What else aren't you telling us?* "Where will we get the charts, maps, and headings?"

"They'll be waiting for you at Prestwick." McBride looked at his watch.

"Have you got a piece of paper?" Linda pointed at McBride. "I want you to call and explain what's happening and where we'll be. It's the number of my brother, Michael Townsend."

McBride reached into a pocket and pulled out a blue envelope. "Write his name and number on the back of this."

Sharon saw that the return address on the envelope was Richmond, Virginia. She handed Linda a pencil.

Two hours later, they touched down at Chièvres Air Base in south-western Belgium. After they shut down the engines, Sharon asked, "How are we doing for fuel?"

Walter had been keeping a running tally of the fuel consumption. "Plenty to get us to Prestwick."

"So we fuel up there before leaving for Goose Bay?" Linda looked out the window at the row of green ambulances with red crosses on their sides and roofs. "How many wounded are we carrying?"

They maneuvered their way out of their seats, walked down the centre of the fuselage, and opened the rear cargo door. A ramp was being rolled up to the side of the aircraft. Four soldiers were already approaching the ramp with one man on a litter. He was covered with blankets and only his face was visible.

He can't be more than eighteen, Sharon thought.

Sharon, Walter, and Linda backed away from the door as one stretcher after another was brought on board. The wounded were stacked two high along either side of the interior of the aircraft.

Linda turned to Sharon. "I'll do the walkaround." She walked down the ramp.

Walter tapped Sharon on the shoulder. "We'd better get started on the preflight checks. I want to make sure I've got the feel of the cock-pit." He followed her to the cabin.

One of the wounded soldiers reached out to touch her sleeve. Sharon looked at the face of a boy with brown hair and blue eyes. He reminded her of her brother Sean. He asked, "Are you flying us home?"

Sharon smiled and nodded. She saw that he was using the only hand he had to grip her clothing. "That's right. In twenty-four hours, you will be back in the States."

"Where you from?" he asked.

"Canada." Sharon touched his hand. "Can I come back and talk after we're in the air?"

The soldier nodded and closed his eyes. "Sure."

Sharon didn't make it back to the cabin until they'd taken off from Prestwick and were well on their way to Goose Bay, Labrador. She could feel the aircraft becoming a little lighter, a little livelier, as they burned off a fraction of the heavy load of fuel. Sharon tapped Linda on the shoulder. "Okay if I take a break?"

Linda opened her eyes and sat up straight. "What?"

Sharon nodded and waited for Linda to slide her seat forward, take a drink from a thermos of coffee, rub the sleep from her eyes, and take a look around. "You have control." Sharon waited to ensure the transition was smooth, then slid the seat back, took off her headphones, and undid her harness.

Walter looked up from his notepad and smiled. Sharon leaned close to his ear in order to be heard over the rattling roar of the four radial engines. "How are we doing with fuel?"

Walter handed her the pad. She looked over the individual engine consumptions, total amount of fuel remaining, and their reserve. "Two hours?" Sharon pointed at what was framed in a box on the paper.

Walter nodded. "That's our reserve. We can make it all the way to Goose Bay if we like."

Sharon nodded, put her hand on Walter's shoulder, and walked toward the back of the aircraft.

The smell hit her. It was a blend of iodine, sulpha, and dried blood. Sharon spotted the wounded soldier she'd talked with before. His eyes were open and he was watching her. She put her hand on his remaining arm and crouched down so he could hear her over the engines.

"You're back." He looked at her and smiled.

"Stretching my legs." Sharon saw that what remained of his left arm was out from under the blanket. The stump was bandaged just above the elbow.

"Still don't know what hit me. One minute I was up. The next I was in the snow and my buddy was screamin' for a medic."

Sharon nodded. "Where you from?"

"San Diego. How about you?"

"Calgary. For the last five years, I've been living in England." Sharon looked toward the tail of the aircraft.

"Calgary?" the soldier asked.

"Just north of Montana." She watched the trio of flight nurses. They wore slacks and battle jackets and moved from patient to patient. The oldest of the three was attaching a bottle of plasma to a hook above a litter near the tail. The other two appeared to defer to her.

"Okay. Gotcha now. I've never been to Canada."

"You'll be there in a few hours. We land in Goose Bay, and then it's on to Montreal." Sharon stood up. "Back in a minute."

She walked toward the nurse who had the short blonde hair. She was a bit stockier than the others, and had eyes that seemed to take everything in all at once. Sharon touched the flight nurse on the shoulder. She felt the tension there.

The nurse turned and frowned. "What?"

Sharon saw the name ROLLINS on the breast of the woman's jacket. "Could we talk for a minute?"

Rollins looked right and left. "Only for a minute."

Sharon led the way to the front of the aircraft to a relatively private space between the cockpit and main body of the aircraft. She stood nose to nose with Rollins. "Anything I need to know?" she asked. "Right now, we can stop off in Reykjavik, Iceland if we need to. I'd prefer to continue on to Goose Bay. I just want to make sure I have all the information before a decision is made."

Rollins pushed back her garrison cap. "We're short of penicillin and morphine. Everyone is. I'm hearing that there may be as many as fifty thousand wounded." She hitched her thumb over her shoulder. "One of the boys lost both legs and has shrapnel wounds. He has an infection. He's the one I'm most worried about. And there are two others who are running hot. They're being closely watched. I have enough penicillin for the next fourteen hours, but no more."

"Do you want me to ask if it's available in Reykjavik?" Sharon asked.

"Yes." Rollins put her hand on Sharon's shoulder, smiled, turned, and went back to her patients.

Sharon returned to the cockpit, maneuvered her way into her seat, and put on her headphones.

Linda glanced left and raised her eyebrows.

Sharon looked at the checklist, found the frequency for Reykjavik, and picked up the microphone. "Reykjavik tower, this is Yankee

Papa Zulu. We're looking for penicillin. Any available?" She could feel Linda's and Walter's eyes on her.

About thirty seconds later, the radio crackled. "Yankee Papa. Negative on the penicillin. Available at Goose."

Sharon took off her headphones and went back into the cabin. She spotted Rollins and tapped her on the shoulder. "According to Reykjavik, Goose is our best bet."

Rollins nodded, then held up her right hand with fingers crossed.

Sharon headed back to the cockpit and checked her watch. *If everything works just right from here on in, we should be okay.*

CHAPTER 29

[SATURDAY, JANUARY 13, 1945]

They landed at Goose Bay just after sunrise. After the hours of transatlantic flight, it was a wonderland of ice, snow, cleared runway, and evergreen trees.

When they taxied in, Sharon switched the radio to ground control. "Goose ground, Yankee Papa requests food, penicillin, and fuel."

"Affirmative for fuel and food. Negative on the penicillin."

Sharon touched the microphone to reply. She felt Walter's hand on her shoulder. He lifted the right side of her headset. "Give me a chance to track some down. Get the nurse to give you a list of what she needs, and I'll see what I can do."

After shutting down the engines and completing their checklist, Linda, Sharon, and Walter filed out of the cockpit.

Sharon watched as the nurses took food and coffee on board. *I don't know how they keep going. We spell each other off and take catnaps. They never seem to stop.* She walked over to Rollins, took her to the cargo door, and walked with her down the ramp. Ahead of them, Walter talked to the driver of an ambulance. The driver nodded, pointed at the passenger door, climbed in the driver's side, started the truck, and drove away.

"See that?" Sharon nodded in the direction of the departing ambulance.

Rollins nodded as she sipped from a stainless steel thermos cup.

"Walter is on the hunt for supplies." Sharon caught a whiff of coffee. "Any more of that around?"

Rollins handed her the cup. "Hold this. I'll be right back."

Sharon looked out over the airfield. She inhaled the crisp air and the scent of pine. She closed her eyes and opened them when she smelled coffee. There was cup under her nose. Sharon and Rollins switched cups.

A Jeep approached. It stopped near the ramp. A man unfolded himself from behind the wheel. He wore a blue uniform and a cap with gold braid across the brim. His hair was grey on the sides, and his jowls seemed to hang over his tight collar. He didn't smile as he approached. He looked toward the nose of the aircraft and stopped. He regarded Sharon and Rollins. "Who's the captain of this aircraft?"

Sharon heard the authority of command in his voice. She said, "Flight Captain Lacey."

"Where is he?"

"You're looking at her, sir." Sharon took a sip of coffee.

"Elliot." He offered his hand.

Sharon shook it. "What can we do for you, sir?"

"I'm afraid I have a problem. We're short of crews, and your replacements won't arrive until tomorrow." Elliot looked at Rollins.

Rollins took a sip of coffee. "These boys can't wait overnight," she said. "I've got one who's fighting an infection and two who are showing early symptoms of it. They'll be dead if we wait for tomorrow. We need penicillin."

Sharon looked across the airfield to see if Walter was on his way back. "My copilot and I've been spelling each other off on the way over. We'll be able to fly the last thirteen hundred miles to Richmond."

"The sooner we get there, the better." Rollins looked at Elliot.

"There is a shortage of medical supplies. We've rationed penicillin at this end. The next shipment is expected tomorrow with the replacement crews." Elliot turned to Sharon. "You're authorized to continue on to Richmond as soon as refueling is completed." He turned, walked away, and climbed into his Jeep.

Rollins waited until Elliot drove away. "No, thank you. I don't want to fly to Virginia with a couple of dead boys on board. That's what will happen if we have to stay here overnight."

"There's a war on, remember?" Sharon smiled.

Rollins laughed. "So I've been told."

"What was he looking at that made him stop after he got out of the Jeep?" Sharon looked at the nurse.

Rollins laughed so hard she almost spilled her coffee. "You mean you don't know?"

"Know what?"

Rollins took her by the elbow and walked her the length of the fuselage until they stood near the nose. She pointed up at the side of the fuselage. "See that?"

Sharon looked at the name *Sunflower II* painted along the nose under the cockpit. "See what?"

"*Sunflower II* means that this is General Eisenhower's personal aircraft." Rollins raised her eyebrows.

"You can't be serious!" *That's what McBride was hiding.*

"What's all the excitement about?" Linda approached from under the wing.

"We've been flying General Eisenhower's C-54." Sharon pointed at the name.

"Oh, that's exciting." Linda moved closer and looked up.

"The problem is that Eisenhower may be wondering where his aircraft is." Sharon sipped her coffee. *Oh, what the hell! As soon as it's discovered I'm pregnant, I'll be grounded anyway.*

"I wondered what McBride was up to. He was extremely nervous when he said he wanted to do something good for a change." Linda looked at Rollins.

"If word gets around, there might be a few reporters at Richmond when we land." Rollins rolled her eyes and shook her head.

"Maybe we should make sure they *will* be there." Linda nodded her head and smiled as if she'd just come up with a wonderful idea. "We'll provide the General with good press in return for the use of his aircraft. I mean, it's only fair, don't you think?"

Sharon felt a sudden wave of nausea. Her mouth filled with saliva. She turned her back on the two women, bent over, and promptly threw up onto the tarmac.

Linda rubbed Sharon's back with one hand and held her ponytail with the other. "Are you able to continue?"

"Are you pregnant?" Rollins asked.

Sharon straightened up, reached for a hanky, wiped her face, and blushed through her nausea.

"You are?" Linda asked.

"I think so." Sharon looked at Rollins. "I'll be grounded if word of this gets out."

Rollins shook her head. "Nobody will hear it from me. You feeling well enough to get us the rest of the way?"

"We'll get you there." Linda rubbed Sharon's back. "Does Michael know?"

Sharon shook her head. "Not yet."

The horn of an ambulance beeped. Sharon stuffed the hanky in her pocket. "Here comes Walter."

The ambulance pulled up next to the cargo ramp. Walter stepped out and went to the back of the truck. He opened the door, lifted two boxes, balanced them on his right knee, and closed the door with his free hand. He walked up to the cab of the truck and nodded at the driver. The pink palm of a brown hand waved out the window of the ambulance as it drove away. Walter walked up the ramp and into the cabin.

Linda turned to Rollins. "Are you able to call anyone in Richmond who can alert the press that Eisenhower's plane is arriving in about five hours?"

Rollins looked at Sharon and frowned.

"If Linda has a plan," Sharon said, "then she'll take care of things when we land. While you make the call, Linda and I can get ready for takeoff." Sharon walked to the ramp, then up and into the cabin. Walter was setting the two boxes near the tail of the aircraft. He turned and faced Sharon.

"How did you manage that?" Sharon pointed at the medicine.

"You knocked at the front door. I knocked at the back. That's how it works sometimes. My friend asked for one box of penicillin and another of morphine on our return trip." Walter looked around the cabin. "Where to next?"

"Richmond, Virginia. Apparently, there's a big veterans' hospital there." Sharon looked up toward the cabin.

"Richmond? Maybe we'll have time for some home-style cooking. Man, I've been craving Virginia ham." He studied Sharon's face. "You look a little pale."

"Upset stomach. Thanks for getting the medicine. You probably saved the lives of a couple of our boys." She nodded in the direction of the soldier with an IV in his arm and a bottle hanging above his bed.

Walter shrugged. "Glad to do it."

They took off twenty minutes later and landed at Richmond in a little under five hours.

Sharon looked out the cockpit window and saw a clutch of photographers. She turned to Linda as they shut down the last engine. Linda nodded and undid her harness. "I need to take care of the reporters. Have you got this?"

Sharon nodded. She went through the final checks with Walter's help and followed Linda a few minutes later. The last two litters were being lifted off as the wounded boys were being eased toward the ramp. She stood next to the open cargo door and looked toward the gathering of reporters and photographers facing Linda.

"Don't you think it's wonderful that General Eisenhower made his aircraft available to bring wounded soldiers home? It just shows you that with Eisenhower, his men come first." Linda lifted her chin as the bulbs began to flash.

"To hell with that!" The voice came from inside the aircraft.

Sharon turned. Once her eyes adjusted to the softer light, she saw Rollins leaning one arm against the fuselage of the aircraft. Sharon recognized the wounded soldier who had needed the penicillin to fight infection.

"We were out of penicillin," Rollins said. "He managed to get some before we left Goose Bay. You're on the mend now. You wouldn't be without his help. You should thank him."

Sharon stared at the top of the soldier's head. His black hair was uncombed and his nose was crooked from being broken. There were stumps under the blanket where feet should have been.

"You think I'm going to thank him? You got another think comin'!" The soldier shook his head for emphasis.

Sharon looked to her left and saw Walter there, backing away from Rollins and the soldier. Walter's face was a neutral mask, but the anger in his eyes gave him away. Sharon moved next to Rollins, put her hand on the nurse's shoulder, and said, "This woman saved your life!" She turned and pointed at Walter. "This man got the medicine for you!" She looked at the corpsmen holding either end of the litter. "Leave this son of a bitch where he is!" She pointed at the young man. "I'll fly him back to fucking England!"

Rollins took Sharon by the arm and pulled her to the front of the aircraft. She nodded at the corpsmen to carry the wounded soldier out of the aircraft, then pulled Sharon closer. "We do what we do to save their lives. We can't do anything about what's in their hearts."

Walter stepped closer and said to Rollins, "You have to understand, she saw a man executed because he was black. He was our friend."

Rollins turned to Walter.

"His name was Edgar Washington. An MP shot him outside a pub. We all went for dinner. There was a fight. Edgar was shot in the chest. The MP got away with murder. She —" Walter pointed at Sharon, "— tried to get the MP charged."

"There's a war on." Sharon watched the wounded soldier being carried down the ramp. "They told me that nothing would be done about Edgar's murder because there was a war on."

"Sharon! Rollins! Walter! Come down!" Linda stood at the bottom of the ramp and winked. Men with cameras smiled up at them. "They want pictures!"

"I don't know if this is such a good idea," Walter said to Sharon.

"Come on." Rollins grabbed each by an elbow. She turned to Walter. "Just pull your cap down over your eyes."

"You can tell them your name is Edgar Washington if you like." Sharon had the odd feeling that her brain was becoming disconnected from her mouth.

Walter looked at her and smiled.

"After the photos, you're coming with me. I know where we can get some first-class grub," Rollins said.

"Umm. . .," Walter said.

Rollins said, "You're coming, Walter."

"But. . .," Walter said.

"After each trip, we go to Maybelle's on Carlisle Avenue. And there's no reason to worry. Come on, we've got a ride." Flashbulbs caught them as they posed at the cargo door. More followed as they felt their way down the ramp. Linda met them at the bottom for another series of photographs. Rollins hustled nurses and crew toward a Deuce and a Half idling around the side of a hangar. "Now all we need is a driver. We've got a three-hour loan."

Sharon smiled at Walter, who climbed into the cab. Rollins got in the passenger side, and the rest of them clambered into the canvas-topped back of the truck.

Sharon watched out the back of the Deuce. It was a warm day for winter, at least warmer than what they were used to, and she enjoyed the passing scenery, even though her mind was numb with fatigue.

The truck stopped in a residential area and parked out front of a white house. They had to walk half a block to a large red brick house on the corner. People in uniform and civilians came and went.

"Maybelle runs the place," Rollins said. "She has the best food around. She has two sons in the service. She and her daughters keep this place going."

They went around back to a one-storey building set in the middle of a half-acre of backyard. The restaurant had windows on all four sides, and the leafless trees were positioned so as to provide shade for the restaurant and the patio in the summertime.

Rollins opened the door and stepped inside. Sharon found herself salivating at aromas that were both familiar and new. A waitress with light brown skin waved them over to table she was clearing. The six of them sat down. Sharon looked around at a crowd of mixed colours who seemed unaware of their arrival and whose eyes remained focused instead on the food in front of them. Walter looked around, then looked at Sharon. She smiled. The smile became a yawn.

"Coffees?" the waitress asked.

Rollins nodded.

"Specials?" The waitress returned with cups and a carafe of coffee. Rollins looked around the table. Linda asked, "What's the special?"

"Chicken, potatoes, grits, and gravy." The waitress made her way around the table, filling coffee cups.

The nurses nodded and smiled. Linda said, "Sounds good to me."

The conversation began to warm up. Rollins turned to Sharon. "What are you going to do after this mess is over?"

Sharon put her coffee down. She shrugged. "I've been. . ."

"She's been thinking about moving back to Canada," said Linda, putting her hand on Sharon's arm. "I'd like to move there too, if that's okay with you."

Sharon felt the renewed warmth of the connection between them and turned to her friend. "What about Honeysuckle?"

Linda leaned back as a steaming plate with half a chicken, mashed potatoes, gravy, and something resembling porridge appeared in front of her. "I think that she is warming to the idea."

Sharon smiled as her plate arrived. She picked up her knife and fork, closed her eyes, then fell face-forward into her grits.

She was partially aware of a flurry of activity around her. A napkin wiped her face. A pair of hands held her by the shoulders.

"Be careful!" said Linda. "She's pregnant."

Rollins said, "It's the middle of the night in England."

"I need a nap after this," said Sharon. She worked on finishing the chicken and mashed potatoes, then slept for fourteen hours.

CHAPTER 30
[MONDAY, JANUARY 15, 1945]

"Linda Townsend!" The man in the blue uniform and cap wore a white moustache which cut a straight line across his upper lip.

Linda sat up straighter. The evening light backlit her red hair. She was across from Sharon in the waiting area of Montreal's Dorval airport. "I'm Linda Townsend."

Sharon shuddered as she recognized the uniform of a telegraph deliveryman. The telegraph man handed Linda a clipboard. "Sign here, please." Linda signed. He handed her a telegram and walked away.

Sharon felt as if someone had opened a door somewhere and sucked all of the other sounds from the building. All that remained was the echo of the man's heels on the floor as he walked away.

Linda looked across at her friend, who stuck her thumbnail under the envelope flap and took time to breathe. The envelope opened. Linda pulled out the message and unfolded it.

Sharon watched Linda's eyes. Linda glanced at Sharon, then read the message again. Linda leaned forward and handed the telegram to Sharon. Linda bent at the waist, rested her elbows on her knees, and put her head in her hands.

DEAR LINDA,

MILTON CARDINAL ALIVE AND SAFE STOP

WAITING AT COTTAGE FOR YOUR RETURN STOP

MICHAEL

Sharon folded the telegram, got up, and sat down beside Linda, who was weeping and shaking. Sharon began to feel light-headed; then she remembered to breathe.

CHAPTER 31
[WEDNESDAY, JANUARY 17, 1945]

Linda fell asleep somewhere south of Iceland. She was curled in a sleeping bag on a makeshift bed behind the Perspex nose of the Lancaster.

Walter sat next to Sharon in the cockpit of the bomber they'd ferried all the way from Montreal. They were on finals for their landing at Lossiemouth, Scotland. The sun was low in the west and at their backs. Sharon eased back on the controls. The heavy bomber was lighter on the controls now that it had burned off most of its fuel. The wheels skipped along the end of the runway. Sharon closed the throttles. The tail began a slow drop until the tail wheel thumped against the tarmac.

Ten minutes later, they clambered out of the rear side door after the long overseas flight that left them with unsteady legs and that old friend, fatigue. They would search first for a washroom, then hot food.

They stood next to the tail of the bomber. Sharon looked at the grey sky. Linda wiped sleep from her eyes.

Walter turned at the sound of an approaching truck. "What the hell?"

The driver's eyes caught Sharon's attention. They were wide and intense under a green wool cap. The passenger wore a US Army Air

Corps brown crusher cap that looked like it had flown more than fifty missions. The truck stopped, the engine idled, and the passenger got out. He wore a sheepskin jacket and a khaki flight suit. His chin was square, his eyes were blue, and his voice boomed. "My orders are to fly the three of you back to London!" He jerked his thumb at the rear of the truck, indicating that they should climb in.

Sharon looked at Linda. Walter stepped forward to do as he was told.

"Who are you?" Sharon asked.

"Captain Markham," the pilot said.

"We're hungry," Sharon said.

"My orders are —" Markham began.

"We need a hot meal." Sharon put her hands on her hips. Her stomach growled, she blushed but stood her ground.

"And I need to powder my nose," Linda added.

Walter hesitated in the no man's land between Markham and Sharon.

Their first stop was the canteen near the washroom. Markham kept glancing at his watch as he drank coffee. He held his cup with both hands and sipped. Meanwhile, Sharon, Linda, and Walter chatted about the flight and the meal they'd eaten in Richmond.

Linda turned to Markham, who was lighting a cigarette from the nub of another. "You seem a bit troubled."

Markham inhaled, then smiled for an instant. "Orders."

"From who?" Sharon asked.

He tipped back his battered cap, blew smoke, and looked at the ceiling.

"God?" Linda asked.

"Higher than that." This time, Markham surrendered a smile that revealed his yellowed teeth.

Sharon leaned back and realized that her gnawing hunger was satisfied for the moment. She lifted her coffee cup and drained the contents. "I'll be back in a minute."

When she returned from the bathroom, the others were waiting at the door. They all went outside into the winter wind and climbed in the back of the waiting truck. This time, Markham sat in the back.

Walter turned to Markham. "How many missions have you flown?"
Markham's eyes went wary. "Two tours. Fifty missions."

The truck took them to a waiting A-26 Invader. Its polished aluminum gleamed despite the hastily applied black and white invasion stripes. The bomber stood poised for flight on its tricycle landing gear. They climbed inside and sat between the wings and the tail. There were small windows in the sides of the fuselage.

Markham went up front. Sharon watched out the window and waited for the engines to start up. She observed as they took off. She felt the wheels lift off the runway. She looked out the window and watched the starboard wheel retract. The Invader climbed with confidence. *Markham knows what he's doing.* Her eyes felt heavy. She closed them for a minute.

She woke up when the A-26 touched down at Croydon.

Within ten minutes, they were in a grey-green Cadillac. Sharon sat back and enjoyed the pleasure of thickly cushioned seats. Linda sat next to her, with Walter on the far side. Markham sat up front and began to smoke. Sharon swallowed her nausea and opened the window. "Put that fucking thing out!"

Markham turned, saw the pale ghost of Sharon's face, and flicked his smoke out the window.

It was a short trip to a building with a control tower sticking up like a nose in the middle of a broad face. The driver led them inside and into a private room.

Sharon saw a group of men with stars on their caps. One moved toward them. He held a cigarette in his hand and smiled as he approached. A man with a camera followed closely behind.

"Eisenhower," Walter said.

Sharon and Linda looked at each other with raised eyebrows.

"I wanted to meet the crew that ran away with my airplane." Eisenhower smiled as he extended his hand. Sharon's stomach grumbled a warning as she shook it.

Eisenhower said, "Thank you for taking such good care of our boys." He stood between Sharon and Linda with Walter at one end. The cigarette smoke rose up and Sharon gagged. Walter patted her on the back.

"Anything I can do for you?" Eisenhower asked as the cameraman raised his camera.

"I'm feeling a bit under the weather. Would you please put that cigarette away?" Sharon asked.

"Of course." Eisenhower handed the cigarette to his adjutant.

"Thank you." Sharon took a deep breath to hold down her last meal.

Linda turned her shoulders and dropped her chin. "Actually, there is something you could do. Walter could use a promotion. You know, he managed to get life-saving medicine for the boys on the plane when we ran out."

"Walter?" Eisenhower asked.

"Yes, Airman Walter Coleman." Sharon cocked her head to the right.

Eisenhower leaned forward and looked at Walter. "I thought your name was Washington."

"A misunderstanding, I'm afraid." Linda's smile disarmed all males within thirty feet.

"I'll see what I can do." Eisenhower straightened up, looked at the camera, and blinked when it flashed. "I'm off to Versailles." He shook their hands again and left ahead of a troupe of servicemen. The three of them were left in an empty room.

Douglas poked his massive head through the open door. "Anyone need a lift?"

Less than half an hour later, they were on finals for White Waltham.

Sharon looked out the window and saw a trio of Jeeps parked along the road leading to the airfield. Each of the Jeeps had a white star painted on its bonnet. Six white helmets were visible, either standing next to the Jeeps or sitting in them. As Douglas taxied up to the hangar, she saw a pair of Canadian military policemen in their red-topped caps. Sharon felt a growing sense of unease. When Douglas shut off the engines, she was the first out the door.

She took in the scene as she walked toward the MPs. The policemen were on either side of Ernie. Both towered over him. One had red hair and the other black. Ernie looked from one to the next.

"Hello." Sharon waited for the heads to turn.

The MPs gave her a "mind your fucking business" look.

"I'm Flight Captain Lacey. What can I do for you gentlemen?" Sharon kept her rage in check while she moved in close so that the MPs would either have to look down at her or back up a step.

"We're taking Mr. Shane in for questioning," the black-haired one said.

"Could I see your orders, please?" Sharon asked.

The MPs looked at one another.

Keep pushing, Sharon thought. "Could I have your names and the name of your commanding officer?"

The redhead took a step back.

Sharon moved closer to the dark-haired MP. "Names, CO, and orders, please." *You boys have cooked this one up on your own!*

The black-haired MP looked down at her. "We don't have to answer to you."

"Oh yes you do," said Linda. "She's the commanding officer here." Linda moved to stand next to Sharon.

"Why are you answering to the six American MPs parked just down the road?" Sharon asked.

The black-haired MP took a step back.

"I want your names and the name of your CO," Sharon said.

The men turned and walked toward a waiting Jeep. Sharon watched them climb in and drive away, then turned to Linda. "Go to the cottage. Milton is there. I'll handle this." She faced Ernie. "What was that all about?"

Ernie looked at his hands. Linda looked over her shoulder at the departing red caps.

"Go." Sharon nodded and smiled at her friend. "We'll be fine." Linda walked toward the dispersal hut.

Walter, Ernie, and Sharon formed a triangle as they stood on the concrete apron just outside the closed hangar door. A chill wind swirled around them. "They said they wanted to ask me some questions." Ernie stood with his hands in the pockets of his grey coveralls.

"What kinds of questions, exactly?" Sharon felt hunger gnawing at her stomach. *Does this baby ever stop being hungry?*

Walter stuffed his hands in his jacket. Ernie shrugged.

"Were they asking about Beck?" Sharon felt the cold on the back of her neck and pulled up the collar of her sheepskin jacket.

Ernie nodded. Sharon waited. Walter hunched his shoulders against the cold.

"No more killing," Sharon said.

"What?" Ernie's eyes opened wide. Walter stared at Sharon.

"You heard what I said. I'd like an answer." Sharon looked from Ernie to Walter. "I'm not asking about details. I think I know those already. Someone put motor oil in the brake fluid reservoir of Beck's Jeep. The American MPs know it. That's why they're after the pair of you. All I want to hear is that there will be no more killing."

Ernie looked at the ground. Walter did the same.

"Well?" Sharon asked.

"No more killing," Walter said.

"No more killing," Ernie said.

"It's cold as hell out here." Sharon walked up to the dispersal hut with her hands in her pockets. She opened the door and spotted Mother. "Well, what else did I miss?"

"How much weight did you lose?" Sharon looked at Milton, whose face was definitely thinner. She looked closer. His clothes appeared to be at least two sizes too big on him.

Milton smiled. "Almost twenty-five pounds."

"You can count his ribs. He definitely needs some fattening up." Linda tapped Milton on the arm.

So you've been counting his ribs, Sharon thought.

"How about supper? My treat." Milton reached for his jacket.

"I've been craving a good feed of fish and chips." Linda looked at Sharon.

Sharon tapped her belly. "Count me in."

They drove into Maidenhead to a small shop with whitewashed exterior walls, a low roof, and the best fish and chips Linda had been able to track down.

I hope the smell of fried food doesn't make me sick. Sharon sat down next to Linda while Milton went to order. "What happened to him?

How did he get back?"

Linda nodded in Milton's direction. "I'd like to hear him tell it again."

Milton sat down and put his hand on the back of Linda's chair.

"Well?" Sharon asked.

"Well what?" Milton smiled.

"What happened, and where have you been?"

Milton looked at Linda. "You want to hear this again?"

Linda nodded.

"We were on patrol near Wiesbaden. I was arse-end Charlie. One moment I was flying along, scanning the sky. There was an explosion. I pushed the stick hard over. Kicked opposite rudder, spun down to twenty thousand feet, recovered, and took stock. There were several holes bigger than my foot in my starboard wing.

"The controls appeared to be fine, so I headed for home. I tried to raise my section leader, but there was no reply on the radio, and my instruments were acting up. The engine temperature was rising.

A bell pinged. Milton turned around and saw that their fish and chips were ready. Linda and Sharon got up.

"My treat." Milton stood up and brought over three baskets of fish and chips.

Sharon took a chip from her basket, popped it onto her tongue, then opened her mouth and inhaled as soon as the heat touched her tongue.

"Go on," Linda said to Milton.

"I knew where I was, but as the engine temperature kept rising, I knew I'd probably have to bail out or crash-land before I could get home." Milton picked up a chip, blew on it, and popped it into his mouth. "I throttled back and hoped the engine would last a little longer. The temperature went into the red. The engine started to make a banging sound, so I feathered it, shut it down, and glided to ten thousand feet. There were trees below, so I pushed back the canopy, undid the harness, bailed out, and landed in a clearing somewhere near Schleiden — near the German border with Belgium." He took a piece of fish in his fingers and held it up like an exhibit. "After two days of walking, I was dreaming about food."

179

"You walked all the way back?" Sharon heard the disbelief in her voice. She watched to see if her words stung Milton.

Linda poked her arm. "Watch it!"

"Don't worry. I thought people would find it hard to believe. I knew I was eighty miles from my base. I had warm clothes and didn't have to worry about water. I had a bar of chocolate, a map, and a parachute. I figured I could walk ten miles a day." Milton picked up another piece of fish. "This tastes wonderful. I can't get over how easy it is to get food here."

Sharon munched on the end of a fillet. *It does taste very good.*

"I was in the woods and walked as far as I could the first night. I wanted to get as far away from the wreck as possible. My grandfather's words kept coming back to me. He always said, 'Bullshit baffles brains.'"

"What did he mean?" Linda asked.

"He meant that I knew where I was, and I knew where I needed to be. All I had to do was walk to where I needed to be. All of the rest — the Germans, the lack of food, being alone, being shot down, the odds against me — was bullshit." Milton stuffed the remainder of the fish in his mouth.

"How come the Germans never caught you?" Sharon picked up a chip.

"Every morning, I'd pick a spot — usually on a hill — where I could see what was going on and plan the next night's trip. I'd wrap myself in the parachute and watch. Because there was snow on the ground and the parachute was white, I knew I was hard to spot. I also stayed off the roads and away from people. Then, at night, I would walk with the parachute wrapped around me. I'd take the route I'd planned out during the day. Sometimes I'd find a bit of food along the way." Milton looked at the remaining chips in Linda's basket. "Are you going to eat those?"

Linda looked at Sharon. Sharon got up and ordered some more chips.

"Did you want these?" Milton looked at Linda while eating a chip.

"Go ahead. Tell us what happened after that," Sharon said.

"When I started to hear heavy guns, I knew I was close to the front lines." Milton ate the last of Linda's chips.

Sharon stood up to get her order. She returned, sat down, looked at Milton, and said, "Half for me and half for you. Now, how did you get through the lines without getting killed?"

"I spent a day on a hill that looked down over a road. It was overlooking the front lines. I could hear small arms fire." Milton took a chip and popped it into his mouth. "The sun was high in the sky when the Nazis began their retreat. There were soldiers sitting on the tanks. So many soldiers that some of them had to stand and hold onto the gun on the tank. The half-tracks were filled with soldiers, too. I was watching them and wondering how soon the Americans would be following them up the road." Milton went to pick up another chip, then stopped.

"You didn't tell me this before," Linda said.

His eyes adopted the thousand-yard stare. "About six Typhoons caught the Germans on the road. The soldiers scrambled off of the tanks and ran into the trees. The Typhoons worked in a figure eight so that while one Typhoon attacked, there was another one getting lined up to fire its rockets or its cannons. One of the rockets hit a tank. The tank started to burn and the crew tried to get out. One guy was on fire. He tumbled out and fell onto the ground. Another guy was halfway out of the turret when the flames boiled out around him. He fell back inside. I've been on strafing runs like that, but I was never close enough to see what happens to the people on the ground. Some of the soldiers were hit by cannonfire. What was left looked more like hamburger than men."

Milton looked at Linda. Linda put her hand on his shoulder. Sharon recognized the expression on his face. *Help him out and change the subject.* "How did you get through the lines?"

Milton's tone changed, became more of a monotone. "I waited until I saw the American tanks coming up the road. By that time, all of the German soldiers were long gone. The Americans just went around the burned-out tank. After that came the GIs and a few Jeeps. The road was empty. I wrapped the parachute around my shoulders like it was a scarf or something, walked down to the road, and started walking away from the carnage. I ended up at some kind of field kitchen. I put my arms up, this GI pointed his rifle at me and asked, 'Who the hell are you?' I told him, 'I'm a fucking Canadian.'

"The guy looked like he hadn't shaved in a couple of days. He lowered his rifle and asked me if I was hungry." Milton looked at the chips. "I don't think I've stopped eating since."

CHAPTER 32
[THURSDAY, JANUARY 18, 1945]

"We need to talk." Sharon stared at the black phone in Mother's office. She toyed with the cord as she spoke into the receiver.

"About what?" Michael asked.

"Face to face." Sharon thought about what he might be doing at this moment. All he would ever say about his work was that he "read the mail."

"I don't see how at the moment. We're short of people. We're gathering information about another horrible mess on the continent."

Sharon heard exasperation in his voice and something else she'd not heard before: rage. "What's happened?"

"We can't talk over the phone."

Sharon said, "Exactly."

"There's a bloody war on!"

Sharon took a breath and forced an artificial calm into her voice. "Yes, there is a war on. Yes, we are husband and wife. Yes, we need to meet face to face. And yes, the war can do without us for an hour or two."

"I'll see what I can do." Michael hung up.

Sharon slammed the phone down. "Shit!"

Mother was writing on his chalkboard when she came out of the office. "There's a meeting tomorrow afternoon at Haddenham.

Commodore D'Erlanger and Commander Gower request your attendance."

Sharon put the back of her right hand to her cheek and felt the heat there.

Mother put the chalk down and faced her. "I was thinking that the Storch needs a trip. It would also require that you leave early in the morning with a stop for breakfast at Bletchley Park."

So you were listening in! Sharon stood on her toes, hugged Mother around the neck, and got a whiff of pipe tobacco. "Thank you."

"This afternoon, I believe Colonel McBride owes you an apology. His MPs exceeded their authority." Mother raised his eyebrows. "You may use my phone again if you like."

Sharon thought for a moment, then raised her index finger. "Would you please phone the good colonel, make sure he's in, and say that I'm on my way?"

"A strategic move?" Mother went into his office to make the call.

Sharon went to get a cup of coffee.

A few minutes later, Mother joined her and poured himself a tea. "Colonel McBride will be expecting you within the hour. He asked what your visit was about, and I told him I was not privy to that information."

"Good." Sharon took a sip of coffee, put the cup down, and reached for her Irvine jacket. "Thank you, Mother. I'm off."

It took a little under an hour to drive to the American base. She parked in front of a pair of pale green Quonset huts. They always reminded Sharon of bean cans buried in the ground with doors and windows cut into one end. She got out of the MG, closed the door, and thought about what she would say to McBride.

She opened the door and went inside the building on the left. A sergeant sat behind a desk. He wore a khaki-coloured uniform and a perfectly knotted tie, and had matching perfect teeth and a well-fed, round face. "Yes, ma'am?"

"Flight Captain Lacey to see Colonel McBride." Sharon took off her Irvine jacket to reveal the blue of her uniform jacket.

The sergeant stood and opened a door to his left. "He's expecting you."

Sharon walked through the door. The sergeant closed it behind her.

Colonel McBride stood. His grey hair was cut shorter than she remembered. The brick wall behind him was decorated with paintings of a knight on a white horse and a damsel having her hand kissed by an admirer. "What can I do for you?"

Sharon was startled by his aggressive tone. She was even more unprepared for what he did next.

He handed her a pad of lined yellow paper and a pencil. Then he held up another pad on which he'd written: THE SERGEANT IS LISTENING. MY PREDECESSOR MADE A POINT OF SURROUNDING HIMSELF WITH BIGOTS. McBride flipped to the second page. BACK HOME, MEN LIKE HIM WOULD HANG A NEGRO FOR ENTERTAINMENT ON A SATURDAY NIGHT. McBride frowned. "Well? Get to the point!"

Sharon thought, *Play along.* "What were your MPs doing at White Waltham yesterday?"

"Their jobs! One of my men was killed! They were there to investigate his death!" McBride turned his palms up to indicate she should raise the volume. He was a conductor in front of a one-person orchestra. "Well? Speak up!"

"You fuckin' Yanks murder one of my men and do nothing. His killer dies in an accident, and you get your Yankee knickers in a knot!" Sharon raised her eyebrows.

McBride nodded and mouthed the word 'better.' "My MPs have every right to question your mechanic!"

Sharon wrote on her pad and held it up. WHAT DO WE DO NEXT? "Like hell they do!"

"You get out of the way of justice!" McBride wrote on his pad.

"The hell I will!" Sharon waited.

McBride held up his notepad. YOU NEED TO TRANSFER SHANE. "I will do whatever the hell I please! You can't protect him forever!"

Sharon wrote as she spoke. "Just watch me!" She held up her paper. YOU NEED TO HAVE WALTER TRANSFERRED TO THE 332ND.

McBride nodded. "Get the hell out!"

"This isn't over!" Sharon turned, dropped the yellow pad on McBride's desk, winked at him, and made sure to slam the door on her way out. She didn't need to fake the glare she aimed at the desk sergeant.

CHAPTER 33
[FRIDAY, JANUARY 19, 1945]

Sharon eased the single-engined Storch over a stand of trees and dropped down onto a pasture running alongside Bletchley Park. From the air, it was a collection of peaked roofs, brick and stone buildings, and manicured grounds. It was west and north of London, a quiet patch in war-ravaged Europe.

The Storch thumped over the uneven ground and stopped. Sharon checked the gauges, shut down the engine, then turned off the switches. She took off her helmet, opened the side door, and stared along the black barrel of a Sten gun.

"Hands up!" The commando behind the machine gun lifted the weapon for effect.

Sharon did as she was told. *Christ, you've landed beside a top-secret installation in a Nazi plane. What the hell were you expecting?*

"Get out!" The commando wore a green beret, cold green eyes, a black moustache, a pair of ammunition pouches, and sergeant stripes.

Sharon climbed out and stood there with her hands up. *Just keep your mouth shut!* Her stomach heaved. She belched.

"Who the hell are you, and what are you doing here?"

"I came to see my husband, Michael Townsend." *Shit! Why can't you keep your mouth shut?*

The commando lowered his weapon and smiled to reveal crooked teeth. "Well, why didn't you say that? Michael said his wifey might drop in some day. Just never said when. And he never said you'd be flying a Nazi crate like this one." He nodded at the Storch, turned, and waved for her to follow. "They used one of those to rescue Mussolini. Didn't work out so well for him in the long run."

Sharon promptly threw up on the grass.

The commando turned back, patted her on the back, and held her ponytail. "Havin' a gun shoved in your face will do that."

Sharon straightened up, spat, and wiped her sleeve across her mouth. *This baby isn't even born, and it's already causing trouble.* "Thank you." She followed the commando to a building that looked like a random collection of bricks, stones, windows, and a silver-green cupola stuck on for added confusion. The metal on the soles of the commando's boots tapped the stone floor as he led her into the front entrance. "The missus is here to see Michael Townsend," he announced. He turned, took Sharon's hand, shook it, and marched out.

The woman at the desk wore a dark grey military jacket and skirt. She stood. "Follow me." The woman's bobbed auburn hair bounced as she went up the stairs to an office. She knocked.

"Come in!" Michael said.

The door opened and Sharon stood face to face with her husband. There were strands of grey in his strawberry blonde hair and dark smudges under his blue eyes. "Sharon?"

There was the sound of retreating footsteps as the woman in grey went back to her station.

"I'm on my way to Haddenham and stopped by to say hello." Sharon felt his arms around her waist as he drew her close and kissed her.

Michael backed away and pulled her inside an office with one solid wall of windows that filled the room with morning light. He shut the door. "Are you feeling all right?"

Sharon put her hand to her mouth. *My breath smells of vomit!* "Sorry about that."

"I must apologize for being so short on the phone. I can understand why you'd want to divorce me. We've hardly spent any time together since getting married." Michael stood in the middle of the room.

He looks like a whipped dog. "Divorced? What are you talking about?" Sharon felt like laughing and crying at the same time.

"That's why you're here, isn't it? You said we had to meet face-to-face. It sounded like an ultimatum."

Sharon saw the tears in his eyes. *The poor guy's miserable. Just tell him.* "I'm pregnant."

Michael frowned, looked to his right, appeared to be doing mental math, and leaned back against his desk. He stared at her with an open mouth. "That's why?"

"Why?" Sharon turned her head to the side. *God, it's hot in here.* She unzipped her Irvine jacket.

"Why we needed to meet. Why we couldn't talk over the phone." His chin fell to his chest. "This is totally unexpected."

"In a good way or a bad way?" Sharon felt a sudden apprehension.

"In the best possible way!" He pushed himself forward and threw his arms into the air. "There have been reports coming in. Horrible things. Things I can't believe even in war. Camps. Exterminations. The numbers are unbelievable. I knew we were fighting a ruthless enemy in the Nazis, but this is worse than even I could have imagined. We'd had inklings of course, but now — now we have the proof." He picked up a folder of photographs, looked at Sharon, and put the photographs back on his desk. "These made me feel there was no hope because the numbers are. . . the numbers are obscene." He looked at Sharon, leaned back, and pushed his right hand though his hair. "You must think I'm mad."

Sharon smiled. "Now that you mention it. . ."

Michael reached for his cigarettes.

Sharon shook her head. "Can we go outside? I get queasy in the mornings, and cigarettes make me nauseous."

Michael nodded.

Sharon moved in close and hugged him. "What do you do here?"

Michael tucked his chin next to her neck. "You know that's a secret."

"I know." She inhaled the scent of him. It was a mixture of tobacco, hair oil, and his special scent.

He put his lips close to her ear. "We read Hitler's mail."

Sharon tried to absorb what he'd just revealed to her. *How?* "Can we go outside?"

Michael grabbed his jacket and followed her down the stairs. The woman at the front desk nodded at them as they passed. Michael and Sharon entered the passageway with the arched ceiling that led outside. They crossed the driveway and walked onto an expanse of grass dotted with trimmed evergreens.

Sharon looked out toward the Storch and caught a glimpse of the commando who was tucked behind a tree and almost invisible. She pointed. "Who's that?"

Michael followed her gaze. "Donald. He's been here for a few months. Fought in North Africa, Italy, and Normandy. Tough as nails. Soft as a baby's hair."

"He met me when I landed," Sharon said.

"Donald doesn't miss much of what happens around here."

Sharon tucked her arm into Michael's elbow. "Neither do you."

"It looks like the Nazis are almost spent. They've all but lost the Battle of the Bulge. The losses on both sides were massive. We can replace our casualties; Hitler cannot. The Russians are closing in from the east, and we're ready to push into Germany from the west. This war could be over by the summer. Just in time for the baby." Michael looked east, as if he could hear the distant pounding of the guns and the clatter of tracked vehicles.

"I sometimes can't remember what it was like before there was war." Sharon looked up at the sky as a pair of Mosquitoes flew at ten thousand feet.

Michael nodded. "Maybe you're right."

"About what?" Sharon faced him.

"Maybe we should move to Canada after this is all over."

There was a copy of the American newspaper *Stars* and *Stripes* sitting on the oak table surrounded by four chairs. The room was inside a small outbuilding at the edge of the Haddenham Airfield. The woman who ushered Sharon into the austere room asked, "Coffee or tea?"

"Coffee, please." Sharon unfolded one of the newspapers.

Beneath the masthead on the newspaper was a headline: "Bringing Our Boys Home: An Allied Effort." Beneath the headline was a photo of Linda, Walter, Sharon, Rollins, and two nurses. Sharon smiled when she saw that Walter was identified as Edgar Washington.

The door opened and Gerard d'Erlanger entered the room. A moment later, Pauline Gower arrived. Gerard had dark hair, a handsome face, and a businesslike approach. Pauline wore slacks, had her hands in her pockets, and kept her hair cut short. She smiled with her trademark gap-toothed grin.

Sharon nodded and stood at attention. "Good afternoon."

"You're looking well, Sharon." Pauline shook hands with her.

Gerard shook hands then sat down at the head of the table. "Glad you were able to meet with us today."

Pauline sat down between Sharon and Gerard.

Gerard pointed at the newspaper in front of him. "You and your crew did yeoman service and provided the ATA with some much-needed publicity. The role played by our pilots is often forgotten."

Pauline tuned to Sharon. "There have been a number of laudatory comments made through channels about the article, and a personal thank you was relayed from General Eisenhower. Apparently, Eleanor Roosevelt was also very impressed by your accomplishment."

"I had a very good crew. Linda Townsend and I shared the flying duties. She also charmed the reporters in America. Walter Coleman was indispensible. He was able to procure medicine that saved at least one life." Sharon felt herself beginning to sweat under the uniform jacket.

"I'm glad you mentioned Airman Coleman. We've had a concern expressed about the involvement of Coleman and Shane in the death of an American sergeant." d'Erlanger checked his notebook. "Name of Beck."

"Beck murdered one of my men." Sharon felt her anger rising. *Keep your mind clear and your voice calm!*

Pauline touched Sharon's sleeve. "Yes, I remember that you made persistent attempts to have Beck charged with the killing of Washington."

Sharon nodded. "Edgar Washington was unarmed and was murdered in front of me."

"A regrettable incident," d'Erlanger said.

"Very." Sharon heard the sarcasm in her voice and felt Pauline's fist punch her knee under the table.

D'Erlanger frowned. "As you can well imagine, maintaining cooperation between the various Allied groups has been a bit of a challenge at times. I would hate to see anything happen that might spoil the goodwill created by your flight to America."

Say it now! "I would recommend that Ernie Shane be promoted and returned to Canada as an instructor. He is a talented mechanic who has managed to safely maintain a variety of aircraft and improve the safety record at White Waltham."

Pauline Gower seemed to tense up, but kept her eyes on d'Erlanger.

D'Erlanger frowned and looked out the window. "A very wise move, I think. Remove Shane from the scene. How about this Coleman?" D'Erlanger pointed at the photograph. "Or Washington. Which is it?"

"Coleman. I've been assured that he will be transferred to the 332nd in Italy," Sharon said.

"I'm not familiar with that group." d'Erlanger studied Sharon.

"A fighter group called the Red Tails who operate out of Ramitelli Airfield." Sharon maintained eye contact with her superior.

"I see. Both will be removed from the scene. A suitably diplomatic solution to a touchy problem, I should think." D'Erlanger stood up. "A very satisfactory meeting." He left the room.

Pauline turned to face her. Sharon thought, *How come he left so quickly?* "Another matter requires his attention," Pauline said.

There was a knock on the door. Pauline stood up, opened the door, and was handed a tray of coffee and tea. Sharon got up and closed the door. She waited as Pauline poured herself a tea. Sharon poured a coffee from the carafe, then added cream and sugar.

Pauline sipped her tea. "I was hoping to hear your perspective on the Lady Ginette Elam situation."

Even in war, the princess must be given her due. "What would you like to know?"

Pauline walked closer to the window. "I understand she left White Waltham quite abruptly."

Sharon stood on the other side of the table. *I know how to fly, but the niceties of British etiquette escape me. Oh, to hell with it!* "Ask me direct questions. My answers will be equally direct."

Pauline turned to her and smiled. "Why did Lady Ginette leave?"

"She made a racist remark about this man. I was a witness to her outburst." Sharon pointed at Walter on the front page of the newspaper. "I said that her fascist leanings were showing."

Pauline blinked.

"I also told her that Walter came to fight the Nazis, while she initially wanted to join them." Sharon sipped her coffee, then went to add a bit more cream.

Pauline stared at Sharon, then began to laugh. "You didn't!"

Sharon took a long breath and shrugged her shoulders. "She was a member of the British Union of Fascists."

Pauline stopped laughing. "You're joking."

Sharon shook her head and sipped her sweetened coffee.

"How did you come by this information?"

Sharon shrugged.

"I was very sorry to hear about the death of your father-in-law." Pauline watched Sharon as she sipped her tea.

Pauline, you are very sharp! "So was I."

"Be careful of Lady Ginette. She still has powerful friends in certain social and political circles."

Sharon took another long breath. "I never have quite been able to understand British society. That's the problem. I see what needs to be done, and then get it done. Afterward I find out that there were protocols to follow."

Pauline shook her head. "After the war is over, some of those same people who were happy to have us risk our lives will expect you and me to stay home and become obedient wives and mothers."

"After this war is over, it's inevitable that things will be different. Too many people have risked everything and survived. It makes us much harder to control. Much harder for us to accept things as they are."

Pauline smiled. "You're an optimist."

Sharon smiled back. "A realist. I didn't fight to become a doormat."

CHAPTER 34
[WEDNESDAY, FEBRUARY 14, 1945]

Sharon landed at RAF Coningsby. It was on the east coast about one hundred miles north of London. The brand new Lancaster was being difficult on the taxiway. Sweat ran down the sides of Sharon's face from the effort of working brakes and juggling engines. She wiped her face in the crook of her elbow once she was finally able to shut down in front of one of the green hangars. She grabbed her kit and scrambled down the length of the fuselage to the rear side door of the aircraft.

"Hello!" A mechanic stood under the wing of the bomber.

Sharon looked at the man, who wore a cap, grey coveralls, and a leather vest. "Afternoon." She climbed out, turned, and walked up to the smaller opening set into the hangar door. She was careful not to trip over the bottom ledge and ducked so that she didn't bang her head on the doorframe. Inside, there were three Lancasters crammed into the building. The hangar smelled of gasoline, oil, and India rubber. She looked down one wall and saw a sign that marked the location of the bathroom. *I'm about to burst!*

She dropped her parachute and bag on the concrete floor, went down the hallway, saw the open washroom door, stepped inside, and locked the door. She had to unzip her Irvine jacket, hang it up, unzip her flight suit, and shimmy out of that. *Hurry!* She sat down on the cold seat. The relief was ecstasy.

"You saw the flames. It was like something out of Dante." The voice was a baritone. It came from a room across the hall from Sharon.

"I saw it. And I saw what the Nazi bombs did to Coventry and London." This voice was a soprano.

"And those Nazi acts of terror unified us," said Baritone. "Now we bomb a German city and unite its citizens against us. We haven't learned a damned thing."

"As far as I'm concerned," Soprano said, "the Germans started the bombing of cities. Now they can find out what it's like to be on the receiving end."

"I can't see how bombing a city like Dresden is going to help us win the war."

"You sound like a fuckin' bolshy. The Nazis started this war. They bombed their way across Europe. Their buzz bombs and V-2s have rained death down upon us. We gave 'em a taste of their own medicine last night."

"Then," Baritone said, "what makes us different from the Nazis if we attack civilian instead of military targets?"

"It's a fuckin' war! Not once around the block in the back seat of a London taxi!"

There was the sound of a slamming door. Footsteps stamped along the hall past the bathroom door and echoed inside the hangar.

Sharon stood up and began the process of putting her flight clothes back on. The zipper felt tighter than normal when it reached her chest. *Christ, my breasts won't fit in here if they get any bigger!*

She walked out into the hallway just as a brown-haired pilot of twenty or twenty-one opened the door across the hall. He frowned, shook his head, and waited for her to precede him down the hallway.

"Thank you." She stopped in the hangar to pick up her gear.

The pilot walked past her and headed for the door.

She saw him again as she stood in line at the NAAFI wagon. She juggled her parachute, her kit bag, a sandwich wrapped in wax paper, and a cup of coffee.

"Here. Let me at least hold the coffee," the pilot said.

Sharon handed over her cup. She set the parachute and her bag against the wall of a hangar and unwrapped the wax paper so that she could get at the contents. "Thank you." Sharon reached for her coffee.

The pilot handed it back to her. "Turner."

Sharon sipped the coffee. "Lacey," she replied and took a bite of sandwich.

"You must have heard us talking," Turner said.

Sharon nodded as she chewed.

"I just don't think bombing civilians is any way to win a war." Turner pulled up the collar of his blue uniform jacket.

"I don't know if it's possible to fight a moral war. War, by definition, is immoral." Sharon looked over at the Lancaster she'd just delivered and wondered what its first target would be.

"I suppose. But that doesn't really address my point."

Sharon saw the duty Anson land. "There's my ride."

"At least you in the ATA don't have to become killers like the rest of us." Turner bent to pick up her parachute.

"Who says I'm not a killer?"

Turner handed her the parachute without a word. Both realized there was no need to say anything. Sharon read the recognition in his eyes. He had figured out who she was.

Douglas taxied the Anson to the White Waltham hangar. Sharon tapped him on the shoulder. "Thanks."

Douglas nodded and smiled.

"Aren't you going to shut down?"

He shook his massive head. "One more short trip."

She walked downhill to the side door, opened it, backed out, turned, and walked right into Walter. They were buffeted by the propeller wash.

"I'm off to join the Red Tails!" Walter hefted a duffel bag onto his shoulder. "McBride arranged this ride for me. I leave tonight for Ramitelli, Italy! Douglas is taking me to Croydon right now."

Sharon hugged him as the air from the propellers pushed her hair into her eyes.

"Thank you!" Walter kissed her cheek. Then he shoved his duffel bag into the Anson, followed it, and closed the door behind him. Sharon walked over to the hangar and watched as Douglas taxied to the runway and took off.

"He's thrilled to be going. I'm going to miss him," Ernie said.

"Me too." Sharon looked beyond and saw a pair of pilots, two women who had been Lady Ginette's followers. They were looking at Sharon and talking behind their hands. She had a flashback to her school days when girls would talk behind their hands when they discovered Sharon didn't have a father. She walked toward the pilots. They turned and walked into dispersal.

"I got my orders today." Ernie followed her.

Sharon turned and studied his face.

"I'm on my way home in a week. Assigned to Lincoln Park Airfield in Calgary. It comes with a promotion." He smiled at her and cocked his head to one side.

"That is good news for you." *But not for me.* She turned toward the dispersal hut.

"Walter says we have you to thank for our transfers."

Sharon waved at Ernie without turning around. *I'm afraid I'm going to start crying.*

She found Mother behind his counter. He had the radio on and was listening to the BBC. Sharon and Mother listened to the announcer's words:

British and US bombers have dropped hundreds of thousands of explosives on the German city of Dresden.

The city is reported to be a vital command centre for the German defense against Soviet forces approaching from the east.

Last night, 800 RAF Bomber Command planes let loose 650,000 incendiaries, 8,000 pounds of high explosives, and hundreds of 4,000-pound bombs in two waves of attack. They faced very little anti-aircraft fire.

As soon as one part of the city was alight, the bombers went for another until the whole of Dresden was ablaze.

"There were fires everywhere, with a terrific concentration in the centre of the city," said one Pathfinder pilot.

An RAF crew reported smoke rising to a height of 15,000 feet.

CHAPTER 35

[THURSDAY, FEBRUARY 22, 1945]

"How is Reginald doing?" Sharon stood in one corner of the White Waltham hangar.

Ernie stood beside her with his Popeye arms crossed. "He's just a kid, but he knows his stuff."

Reginald Kelly stepped through the open hangar door. He was taller than either Sharon or Ernie, his hair was black and he had a longish, royal nose. He wore white surgical gloves.

"Doesn't like to get grease under his fingernails," Ernie said out the side of his mouth.

"Reginald?" Sharon began to walk toward the nose of the Storch. Ernie followed.

Reginald nodded and walked toward them. "Yes, Flight Captain Lacey?"

"You all set to take over tomorrow?"

He stood at ease with his arms linked behind his back. "I believe so. What is your assessment, Mr. Shane?" Reginald turned his focus to Ernie.

"If you could be a little less fucking formal, things would be just fine."

Reginald blinked. "My school chums call me Reggie."

"I'm Sharon."

Ernie smiled and offered his hand. "That's more like it."

Reggie peeled off his surgical glove and shook Ernie's hand, then offered it to Sharon. "I hear congratulations are in order."

Out of the corner of her eye, Sharon saw Ernie shake his head. Reggie looked from Ernie to Sharon. "I just meant that you look very healthy. Glowing, as a matter of fact."

"Well. Thank you, Reggie. I'll be off, then." Ernie headed for the hangar door. He leaned over and picked up his toolbox. Sharon followed him out. "Let me help with that."

"Not in your condition," Reggie said.

"I'll be fine," Ernie said.

"I'll walk with you." Sharon dogged Ernie as he went around the side of the hangar to a waiting Jeep. Its springs sagged as the weight of the tools settled into the area behind the seats.

"He has a big mouth, too," Ernie said.

"What was that all about?" Sharon faced Ernie and saw the red of embarrassment on his cheeks and forehead.

"Some of the pilots were talking. You know what it's like around the hangar. Lots of people gossip, and they think mechanics are deaf." Ernie shoved his hands into his pants pockets.

Sharon nodded and waited. *Let him fill in the details.*

"Couple of lady pilots from Lady Ginette's crowd." Ernie looked around nervously.

Sharon crossed her arms. "Spit it out, Ernie."

"Pike and Dixon were talking about you and Walter. How you flew together to the States. And there's been talk that you're pregnant. It was about that." Ernie looked as if he wanted to be anywhere but there.

"Oh," Sharon said.

"I owe you. I owe you for getting me out of here before those crackers could get a hold of me." Ernie faced her.

"Crackers?"

"That's what Walter and Edgar called the MPs. And I owe you because you figured out what happened to Beck and didn't turn me in." Ernie put his fists on his hips.

"I'm sure I don't know what you're talking about." Sharon smiled. "Just make sure that you keep your promise."

"No more killing?"

Sharon nodded. "That's right. And when you get home, have some saskatoon pie and tell me all about it in a letter. God, I miss saskatoon pie."

"But what about Lady Ginette's crowd?" Ernie asked.

"What about them?" Sharon leaned against the side of the Jeep.

"They're a nasty bunch. Who's gonna watch your back?" Ernie tapped a forefinger on the metal top of the toolbox.

Sharon looked at the dispersal hut. "You think I can't handle them?"

"I think they're vicious," Ernie said.

Sharon nodded. "Harry — Michael's father — said I was more than a match for that crowd. I've lived through five years of this war. Don't you worry about me."

CHAPTER 36

[MONDAY, MARCH 19, 1945]

"Where's Milton?" Sharon asked when she walked into the kitchen at the cottage.

Linda looked up from her cup of tea. Her eyes were red.

"What happened?" Sharon began to feel that familiar tension arriving the moment before bad news is delivered.

"He's gone. They called him back. He starts training on Tempests tomorrow morning." Linda dropped her chin into her housecoat.

Shit! It seems I'm delivering a Tempest every day to the continent. The losses are very high. Sharon put her arm around Linda's shoulder. "Do you want to go out?"

Linda shook her head. "Do you want to know what's especially pathetic?"

Sharon waited.

"I was hoping I might be pregnant, but I found out when I got home that I'm not." Linda began to weep. She tried to speak and could not.

Sharon held Linda close as her friend's body was ripped by sobs.

Five minutes later, Linda said, "I thought I lost him once. I don't want to lose him again."

CHAPTER 37

[SATURDAY, MARCH 31, 1945]

Mother lifted the phone receiver and held it in the air. He caught Sharon's eye. "Call for you."

Sharon switched her glass of milk to her left hand and took the receiver with her right. "Lacey."

"McBride. You busy over there?"

"It's kind of slow for a Saturday. In fact, we're ahead on deliveries for a change." Sharon took a sip of milk.

"Good. I'll pick you up in thirty minutes." McBride hung up.

Sharon handed the phone to Mother. He hung it up. "Headed somewhere?" he asked.

"Apparently."

"It's difficult to adjust to you drinking milk instead of coffee." Mother smiled at her.

Sharon nodded.

"I also wanted to ask a favour." Mother crossed his arms and leaned against the wall.

Sharon waited.

"I'd like to go along on a trip sometime before the war is over." Mother began to blush.

"When?"

"When you need an extra pair of eyes or you have room for a passenger." Mother looked out the window.

"It would be my pleasure. Do you want to come along today?"

"No, not today. What I'd really like is a ride in a Mosquito or a Lancaster."

"Okay." *I hope I'll be able to deliver on this promise.*

McBride's grey-green Buick with the star on its side drove up exactly twenty-five minutes later. She walked out into sunshine, budding leaves, and songbirds. An American sergeant who wasn't a day over nineteen opened the rear door for her. She climbed into the back seat with McBride.

Colonel McBride smiled. "Something has come up, and I need an expert's input."

"Where are we going?" Sharon asked as the sergeant climbed into the front seat and drove the Buick away from White Waltham.

"Croydon."

"Why not fly?"

"It's a pleasant day for a drive, I think. It's only about fifty miles. We should be there in an hour." McBride pulled a pack of cigarettes out of his pocket.

"Do you mind not smoking, please? I haven't been feeling well." Sharon watched McBride's reaction.

He stuffed the cigarettes back in his pocket. "A disgusting habit, anyway. My wife says the same thing."

It took more than an hour to reach Croydon while traveling along English roads through a series of towns along the southwestern edge of London.

When they approached Croydon airfield and passed the guard post, McBride said, "Things have been going well. The ground troops have invaded Germany, Berlin's air defences grow weaker every day, and there hasn't been a rocket attack since last Tuesday in Kent. It looks like we might be nearing the end of the war. I wanted you to see what a German test pilot brought us."

The sergeant parked in front of a massive white Bellman hangar. The building's wide front doors were closed. MPs armed with submachine guns stood at each corner.

Two of the MPs saluted as Colonel McBride climbed out of the Buick and led Sharon to a side door. An MP opened the door for McBride, and Sharon followed him inside. The door closed behind them.

Sharon's eyes gradually adjusted to the light. Several aircraft were parked inside. One was a Focke Wulf TA 152 crouching on its wide-stance landing gear. Beside it was a Messerschmitt 262. It was silver with black crosses. The jet reminded Sharon of a shark. "I've heard about these, but I've never seen one." She walked closer to the jet to inspect the wing and tail surfaces, then the Jumo engines. She stepped up onto the wing and looked down into the open cockpit. She looked at McBride. "This one is a two- seater."

"A test pilot named Hans Fay defected and landed it at Rhein-Main Frankfurt. I thought you might want to take a look." McBride stood near the nose of the jet.

"It's fast. Only the Meteor can come close to matching its speed, and we have very few of those." Sharon studied the controls.

"Do you believe in symbols?" McBride asked.

"How so?" Sharon looked along the nose of the fighter.

"I think this was a symbolic act. Fay knows the war will be over soon. He disobeyed orders and flew this jet to us so that he could be with his family."

Sharon nodded. *That makes sense.*

"This jet is the best the Nazis have, and Fay just handed it over to us. It looks like we can begin to think about what to do when the war is over."

Sharon looked down at McBride. "Why did you show this to me?"

"My wife and my daughter told me to." He looked up at her, and she could see that his eyes were brimming with tears.

Sharon went to open her mouth and closed it.

"My son-in-law comes from San Diego. He's a first lieutenant. He was wounded at Bastogne. He lost most of his left arm."

Sharon had a quick flashback. She saw the smiling face of the young man whose litter was up near the cockpit of the C-54. *The soldier who said he was from San Diego.*

"He told my wife and my daughter that the crew that flew them home was unusual. The pilot and co-pilot were women, and the engineer was coloured. He said the pilot threatened one of the wounded men who insulted the engineer. My son-in-law said, 'She gave the biggest asshole in the unit a piece of her mind. We've been reminding him of that fact ever since.'"

"What is his name?" Sharon felt a smile spreading across her face.

"Bill." There was a tremor in McBride's voice.

"How is he doing?"

"He's back on his feet, and my daughter is smiling again. Bill told them that you wouldn't leave them until they made it back home. That some wing commander told you that the boys would have to wait over night in Goose Bay for a relief crew. But you decided to fly our boys home."

Sharon nodded and smiled.

"He just got his new arm."

"That is very good news." Sharon blinked and wiped the back of her hand across her eyes.

"And they said I have to take you out for dinner to say thank you from them. I know a great little restaurant on the way back."

"Is it okay if we meet Linda there? She was the co-pilot and she needs some cheering up." Sharon turned to step down off the wing.

"If I could tell them that I took two of the crew out for dinner, it would definitely get me in their good graces."

"Make sure that you mention you got a promotion and a transfer for Walter. You'll get an even better reception when you get home." Sharon stepped away from the jet fighter and wondered what would happen to it when the war was over.

CHAPTER 38
[SATURDAY, APRIL 14, 1945]

Sharon could feel the emotions of shock, anger, and resolve in the mess the afternoon she returned to White Waltham after the delivery of a Tempest to Volkel Airfield in Holland. She had looked for Milton, but did not see him. *That will be the first question Linda will ask tonight.*

Douglas walked beside her. "Do you want a coffee?"

"I think I'll stick to milk." *It helps settle my stomach. A full week without morning sickness. Yes!*

"Grab us a seat. I'll get you a glass," Douglas said.

Sharon looked around and found a pair of empty chairs across from Mother. "Mind if I join you?"

Mother looked up and smiled. "What news do you bring from Holland?"

"Civilians in Nazi-occupied Holland are starving." She sat down. *I sound as bleak as I feel. Isn't it my job to cheer everyone up?*

"Nothing but good news these days." Mother picked at the mutton and beans on his plate.

Reginald dipped a morsel of bread into his beans. He sat beside Mother. Sharon felt a sudden craving for beans on bread.

Douglas sat down with a cup of tea for himself and a glass of milk for Sharon.

"What news have you heard?" Mother asked.

"Probably the same news you've heard. The Americans liberated some camps with names like Nordhausen, Dora, Buchenwald." Douglas stared at the bottom of his cup. "The pictures and the stories are beginning to circulate."

"That's what we're hearing from almost all of the pilots. As our troops move into Germany, they're discovering more death camps. Apparently, there are so many bodies that bulldozers are being used to bury them." Reginald looked at his plate, then pushed it away.

"At Volkel, there was talk of little else." Sharon put down her glass of milk. "The people in the camps have to be put on a special diet because they've been starved and can't eat regular food yet." She noticed Linda pulling up a chair to sit with them.

Other pilots began to do the same.

Mother turned to Sharon. "Are you sure you don't want something to eat?"

Just keep playing dumb. Don't let on that I'm pregnant. They know it and they want to take care of me, but we have to play this game where everyone can deny knowing for certain that I'm pregnant. "I'd love some beans on that fresh bread I caught wind of when I came in the door."

Mother got up.

Linda asked, "Anyone else been reading today's papers?"

This is what Michael was trying to tell me went I went to visit him at Bletchley Park. Sharon turned to her left as a plate of beans on two slices of fresh bread arrived. *I feel guilty being able to eat this.* "Thank you, Mother."

As if reading Sharon's mind, Linda said, "You've had a long day, and you need to eat." Linda looked around the table. "Don't worry about the beans; we sleep in separate rooms!"

The laughter was overloud relief following the grim news of the Nazi concentration camps.

"She toots her own horn?" Reginald asked.

"More like a foghorn. Ships have been known to steer away from our little cottage," Linda said.

Sharon began to laugh, then found herself looking around the room, hoping to see the faces of Edgar, or her father Patrick, or Molly, or Harry.

"I hate to interrupt this line of thought, but I have heard rumours of a Ju 88 being shot down by our windy commander." Mother raised his tea in salute to Sharon and Linda.

Sharon pointed at Linda. "She was the brains of the team."

"Rubbish." Linda pointed at Sharon. "She shot out one of Jerry's engines, and then the other. Her shooting was so precise that the German observer thanked her for not killing him. The pilot, on the other hand, refused to acknowledge Sharon when he was told she shot him down! It must have been a huge blow to his ego to discover he'd been shot down by a woman!"

Linda pulled her hair back with one hand and buttoned up her collar with the other. She stuck two fingers under her nose to approximate a moustache. "The pilot turned his back on us and tried to walk away, but there was nowhere to go, since he was under guard. So he was forced to turn back around and face Windy!" Laughter erupted around the table.

"How many does that make now?" Mother asked.

Sharon drew her hand across her throat.

"No. He won't be quiet," Linda said. "My brother was there when she downed the Me 110. She was flying a Lysander and put the bastard into the ground."

"Then there was the buzz bomb," Mother said.

"Edgar told me how to do that," Sharon said.

"So it's true! That's the first time you've admitted to that one," Mother said.

"So, how many is it?" Linda asked.

Sharon heard the room go quiet. "Ten."

"Christ!" Reginald said.

They all looked at Reginald. Douglas said, "That's the first time we've heard you curse."

"How come no one knows about this?" Reginald asked.

Mother pointed his cup at Sharon. "It's because she's kept quiet about it. And we do the same. Besides, the gentler sex is not supposed to be capable of such acts."

"Rubbish," one of the female pilots said.

"But you're an ace twice over," Reginald said.

Sharon shrugged and put a forkful of beans and bread in her mouth.

Linda sighed. "I'll have to sleep with a pillow over my head!"

Douglas lifted his cup. "Cheers to spring and open windows!"

CHAPTER 39
[SATURDAY, APRIL 28, 1945]

Sharon returned from Rheine Airfield in northwestern Germany, just across the Dutch border. The duty Anson dropped her off at Chadderton near the west coast of England. Her next delivery was a Lancaster bound for the east coast of England.

She stood in line at the NAAFI wagon. Her mind was filled with images of vast expanses of Holland underwater. That, and some of the liberated towns and cities she'd flown over. They'd been bombed and shelled into rubble as the Allies advanced. *I wonder how many cities in Europe aren't destroyed?*

The woman running the NAAFI wagon smiled at her. "What can I get you, love?" She wore a blue Woman's Auxiliary Air Force uniform and cap, and a tired smile.

"Coffee, please."

"You're a polite one." The woman handed her a cup and pointed her in the direction of the cream and sugar.

"What happens when you mix coffee and cream?"

Sharon recognized the voice. She turned to face Lady Ginette, who was behind her in line. Ginette wore an immaculate white flight suit accented with a silver-blue scarf.

"I think the colour is called jigaboo." Lady Ginette smiled and looked around for support.

Sharon shrugged. "Let's find out." With a flick of the wrist, the coffee in Sharon's cup splashed the front of Lady Ginette's white flight suit.

Ginette looked down at the brown stain on her left breast as it bled down to her left knee. "Look at what she's done to me!"

"You're lucky she didn't knock you about a bit. That's what I'd a done if you'd said it to me." The WAAF turned to Sharon. "How about a refill, love?"

Ginette glared at Sharon. Then Lady Ginette's eyes narrowed when she saw Sharon's belly. Ginette smiled.

Sharon landed the new Lancaster on the east coat of England at RAF Scampton. She taxied and stopped in front of a green two-storey hangar. Then she shut down each of the four Merlin engines. In the quiet, she looked over at the grave of a dead hero's dog.

This is probably your last flight, she thought. For most of the trip to Scampton, she'd thought about the look on Lady Ginette's face. *I'm starting to show, and right now she'll be on the phone to one of her influential friends, asking why a pregnant ATA pilot is being allowed to fly.*

She grabbed her gear and began the meandering journey down the fuselage of the bomber to the rear door. A man with thinning combover hair was waiting. The rings of an air commodore adorned the sleeves of his blue jacket. *Lady Ginette works fast.*

"So, I've got a new plane, and now I need to find a crew to fly it," the Air Commodore said.

"Who are you, and what do you need?" Sharon asked. *He needs a crew?*

"Name's Geddes. And you?"

"Lacey."

"I've got two crews on leave, another one that needs a rest, and Operation Manna starts tomorrow." Geddes stuffed his hands into his trouser pockets.

"What if I can gather a crew?"

"Who will fly it?" Geddes turned his head to the side and studied her.

Just keep your mouth shut. She smiled.

"Sharon Lacey, the Canadian?"

She nodded.

"Could we talk inside? It's warmer." Geddes turned and began to walk toward the canteen.

Sharon fell into step beside him. "What's Operation Manna?"

"You've heard that the Dutch trapped behind German lines are starving?" Geddes turned his head toward her.

Sharon nodded.

"We're getting together with the Americans to drop food into Holland." They reached the canteen. Geddes opened the door for her. Sharon stepped inside where it was warm. It smelled of good food and hot coffee.

In less than ten minutes, Geddes began tucking into a plate of bangers and mash. Sharon's mouth watered as she stared down two eggs, bacon, toast, and a cup of coffee.

Geddes cut a sausage into four neat bits. "We're guaranteed safe passage, as long as we stick to specified corridors. That's why you'll need a navigator." He popped a quartered sausage in his mouth and nodded to his right.

Sharon looked to her left and saw a round-faced man sitting with an empty plate in front of him. He was so engrossed in a book that he appeared not to notice anyone else in the room.

"Name's Meron Chorny. Bloody great navigator." Geddes stabbed another quarter of sausage.

"Where's his crew?" Sharon wiped yolk from her chin. *This baby has turned me into a glutton.*

"Off at the nearest pub getting rip-roaring drunk, I suspect. Ask him if he'll fly with you. He's been awfully quiet since Dresden. Doesn't think much of Bomber Harris' claim that the city was a military target." Geddes chewed, then sipped his tea.

"What about a bombardier?" Sharon wrapped a piece of bacon in a wedge of toast.

Geddes lifted his chin and looked behind her. Sharon turned and spotted a light-haired man whose left arm was in a cast.

"Mr. Sutherland. A moment, please," Geddes said.

Sharon turned back around and heard the scrape of a chair on the floor. A moment later, a man sat down gingerly beside her. "Yes, sir?" There was an Edinburgh burr in his voice.

Sharon looked at Mr. Sutherland, who appeared to be a week or two over eighteen. His hair was the colour of sand and he shifted uncomfortably, as if the damage to his arm were only a fraction of the harm that had been done to him.

Geddes nodded at Sharon. "I have a pilot and she needs a bombardier for tomorrow."

Sutherland looked at Sharon. She read his mind.

"I'm supposed to risk my life with a fookin' woman for a pilot, sir?"

Sharon felt her face redden. *Don't piss me off. Not when I'm pregnant.*

Sutherland turned to Geddes. "Are you giving me an order, sir?"

Geddes shook his head. "The Dutch are starving and we have an aircraft without a crew. We need a bombardier who can drop the load from two hundred feet onto a racecourse."

"I see, sir." Sutherland lifted his injured forearm onto the table and looked around the room.

"Do you remember that incident last November? A pilot shot out both engines of a Junkers 88 night fighter so it had to land at Church Fenton. The Nazi pilot was put out he'd been shot down by a woman. The story made the rounds, if I recall." Geddes cut another sausage into four equal bites.

Sutherland looked sideways at Sharon. "You?"

Sharon nodded as she chewed toast and bacon.

He offered his hand. "Call me Willy."

She swallowed and shook his hand. "Sharon."

"You gonna ask Chorny to navigate?" Willy directed the question at Sharon.

"Me?" Sharon picked up another slice of toast and put two bits of bacon in the middle.

"You're the pilot," Willy said.

Sharon stood up with her bacon sandwich. "Be right back."

She walked around the table toward the navigator. She read the name T. S. Eliot on the spine of his book.

"Hello." Meron Chorny's voice was soft, just audible.

Sharon saw his brown eyes and the intelligence behind them. "I need a navigator to guide us into Holland for food drops."

Chorny marked his page with a strand of red yarn. "Willie said he'd fly with you?"

Sharon nodded.

"Food drops?" Chorny's nose whistled as he inhaled.

"That's correct."

"You are the pilot?"

Sharon nodded.

"Any good?" Chorny's eyes locked on hers.

She nodded.

"Why didn't you kill the crew of the Junkers?"

"You were eavesdropping?" she asked.

Chorny nodded.

"I don't want to kill anymore." Sharon heard the bleak honesty in her voice.

Chorny stood up. "Anymore. What an interesting way to put it."

"Well?" Sharon saw that they were about the same height.

"I assume we have to prepare for an early morning mission." He nodded in the direction of Geddes and Sutherland. "I'll need to check the specifics on weather and destination."

"How come you're saying yes?" Sharon asked.

He smiled. "I'd much rather drop food than bombs."

Sharon led the way back to the table, where she sipped her coffee and listened as Willy, Chorny, and Geddes discussed the details. They listened intently when she added her tuppence.

Willy said, "We could use an observer in the tail gun."

"Why?" Sharon asked.

"Someone to evaluate the drops. See if they're short or long." Willy tucked his cast up against his chest.

"I can get one here in two or three hours." Sharon stood. "Where's the nearest phone?"

Mother arrived in time for supper. "Pauline Gower is looking for you."

"And?" Sharon asked.

"I left Linda in charge. She told me she didn't want to know where you are so that she wouldn't have to lie. Only I know where you are." Mother smiled.

Sharon turned to Chorny and Willy. "This is Mr. Green."

Chorny and Willy looked at Mother's grey hair and sparse frame.

"This will definitively get me sacked, and it might do the same for you," Sharon said.

Mother smiled. "It had to happen sometime. What's my job?"

Chorny and Willy looked at one another and smiled. "What's your first name?" Willy asked.

Mother looked at Sharon. "Hubert."

"We call him Mother," Sharon said.

"Mother it is," Willy said.

Chorny pointed. "Mother. You'll have our backs."

CHAPTER 40
[SUNDAY, APRIL 29, 1945]

"Three minutes to target," Chorny said.

Sharon looked ahead through the Lancaster's greenhouse canopy. She checked her altimeter: four hundred feet. She dropped the landing gear and added flap to slow the bomber down for the drop. The ground was snow-covered and the trees were grey arms against that white background. Rooftops spread out below them as they crossed over a beach. Sharon saw antiaircraft guns pointed up at them. They did not fire.

She looked ahead, saw the oval track near another beach, and touched the microphone button. "Target in sight."

"Got it," Willy said. "Fly straight down the middle of the track."

Sharon applied a bit of right rudder and power. They were twenty knots above stalling speed.

"Steady on," Willy said.

Sharon aimed down the middle of the racecourse. *Hope we hit this right. If the drop is long, all of the food will end up in the water.*

She felt the bomb bay doors open. The bomber lifted as the bags of food fell out.

"Food away!" Willy said.

Sharon turned toward the North Sea.

"How'd we do?" Willy asked.

Mother answered from his position in the tailgunner's turret. "In the middle of the course. Almost dead centre."

"Long or short?" Willy asked.

"Perhaps twenty yards long," Mother said.

"Next one will be dead centre," Willy said.

"I'm bushed." Chorny gave his face a wipe with the palm of his hand. "Three trips in one day." He looked around the Scampton mess and smiled. "I thought I was going to have a nice quiet few days of reading."

Mother leaned forward and rested his head in his hands.

"Did you see the people watching us as we flew over Amsterdam? On the last trip, there were people waving and shouting. We were so close, I could see the smiles on some faces." Willy grinned as he lifted his tea in a salute to the other three.

"Want to do it all over again tomorrow?" Sharon asked.

Mother lifted his head and smiled.

Chorny nodded. "Of course."

Willy looked at the other three. "Most fun I've had in years."

CHAPTER 41
[MONDAY, APRIL 30, 1945]

Sharon opened the four throttles and released the brakes. Weighed down by a full load of food, the Lancaster only accelerated gradually. It was sluggish and heavy on the controls as it lifted off. Sharon waited until they were two hundred feet off the ground before retracting the wheels and gradually streamlining the aircraft.

The pink of the rising sun was on Mother's face when she glanced over. His grin was wide. He tapped her on the shoulder, then headed to the tailgunner's position.

This time, the Dutch were waiting for them in force as they flew toward Valkenburg Airport. They were south of Amsterdam and nearing the city of Leiden. Sharon began her approach over the Dutch coast at four hundred feet.

"Four minutes to target," Chorny said.

"You need to see this," Willy said. "Come up here, Chorny. The people are waving at us! The bleeding Nazis have dragged out all of their flags, but all of the Dutch people are in the streets and parks, thanking us!" He took a breath. "Do you have the target in sight, Lacey?"

Sharon peered ahead and saw the lopsided X of Valkenburg's runways. "Dead ahead." She dropped the landing gear to slow the Lancaster down as much as possible. *Too much speed and the food parcels will disintegrate when they hit the ground.*

"Target acquired," Willy said. "Two degrees to port."

Sharon carefully played with the rudders to allow for the wind. The Lancaster rose up as tons of food sacks cascaded toward the intersection of the runways.

"Perfect," Mother said.

Sharon retracted the wheels and brought the aircraft around to head home. She glanced down and saw people waving. She caught a glimpse of two people holding up a blue bedsheet like a flag. Broad smiles. Children jumping. A mother holding an infant.

Then they were over the coast and headed home to pick up another load.

Trouble arrived when she began the engine prestart checks for the third run of that day.

A hand patted her on the shoulder. She looked right into the face of Gerard d'Erlanger. Sharon blinked.

"How many months pregnant are you?" he asked.

"Four."

He nodded. "I have to insist that you come with me." D'Erlanger used his index finger to signal her to follow.

Sharon shook her head. "We've got a load of food to drop."

"I must insist that you leave the aircraft." D'Erlanger lifted his chin for emphasis.

"What are you going to do? Carry me out of here?" Sharon met d'Erlanger's eyes.

He took a long breath. "I won't leave this aircraft without you."

Sharon pressed the microphone button. "Is the rear door closed and locked?"

"I'll check," Mother said.

Sharon turned to finish her checks. "I can guarantee that you'll thank me after we land."

D'Erlanger put his left hand on the back of the pilot's seat.

Sharon slid open the side window. "Fuel on three!"

The mechanic on the ground stuck his finger in the air and made tiny circles. Sharon started the first engine.

"What do you want me to do?" d'Erlanger asked.

"Be another pair of eyes both inside." She pointed at the gauges. "And outside."

D'Erlanger nodded. He stood there, with one hand on the back of Sharon's cushion and one hand on the edge of the cockpit, all the way across the English Channel.

Sharon spotted the waves breaking on the Dutch coast and turned to d'Erlanger. "You might want to join Willy in the nose!" D'Erlanger cupped his left ear and frowned. She pointed toward the front of the aircraft. "*Nose!*"

D'Erlanger nodded and made his way down to the bombardier's position.

"Four minutes to target," Meron said.

"You've got a visitor, Willy," Sharon said.

"Confirmed," Willy said.

Sharon concentrated on the drop and caught a glimpse of waving arms and smiling faces on the approach to the airfield.

She didn't see d'Erlanger again until after they landed at Scampton. She stepped out the rear door of the aircraft. He was there with Mother, Chorny, and Sutherland at the bottom of the ladder. All four were smiling.

"Well, Lacey, should we call it a day?" Willy asked.

Sharon looked west. The bottom edge of the sun was touching the horizon. *My last trip for a while, and I'm too tried to argue anymore.* "Guess we'd better get some supper."

CHAPTER 42
[MONDAY, MAY 8, 1945]

Sharon cleared the cobwebs from her head with a sip of Honeysuckle's coffee. Meanwhile, Sean fiddled with the dials on the radio on the kitchen counter.

Honeysuckle asked, "Are you feeling like you've caught up on your sleep yet?"

Sharon smiled and set the cup down. "I must have been more tired than I thought. I haven't lifted a finger since I got back. You must think I'm a lout."

Sharon felt a brushing against the inside of her belly. She sat up and put her hand to her navel.

"The little one's kicking?" Honeysuckle asked.

"Is that what it is?" Sharon took Honeysuckle's hand and placed it on her belly.

They spent the next few minutes chasing a moving child who kept them playing a mime routine around Sharon's navel.

Honeysuckle's eyes got wide and she smiled. "Yes, that's what it is!"

Sean said, "I'm turning up the radio."

Honeysuckle looked out the door as if waiting for someone to knock or walk through. Sharon stood up and put her arm around her mother-in-law's shoulder.

The BBC radio announcer began to speak:

THE PRIME MINISTER, WINSTON CHURCHILL, HAS OFFICIALLY ANNOUNCED
THE END OF THE WAR WITH GERMANY.

IN A MESSAGE BROADCAST TO THE NATION FROM THE CABINET ROOM AT
NUMBER 10, HE SAID THE CEASEFIRE HAD BEEN SIGNED AT 0241 YESTERDAY
AT THE AMERICAN ADVANCE HEADQUARTERS IN RHEIMS.

HUGE CROWDS, MANY DRESSED IN RED, WHITE, AND BLUE, GATHERED
OUTSIDE BUCKINGHAM PALACE IN LONDON AND CHEERED AS THE KING,
QUEEN, AND TWO PRINCESSES CAME OUT ONTO THE BALCONY.

EARLIER, TENS OF THOUSANDS OF PEOPLE LISTENED INTENTLY AS THE KING'S
SPEECH WAS RELAYED BY LOUDSPEAKER TO THOSE GATHERED IN TRAFALGAR
SQUARE AND PARLIAMENT SQUARE.

"I wonder when we'll see Michael, Linda, and Milton?" Honeysuckle
asked.

Sean said, "Shh! There's more."

Sharon sipped her coffee. She felt that familiar itch. The yearn-
ing to be flying again. For a moment, she heard the hum of an aircraft
engine. Then the baby kicked. *Will it be a boy or a girl?*

ACKNOWLEDGEMENTS

Bruce: for caring for us all these years, thank you. And thank you to Shameem.

Again, thanks to Tony Bidulka and Wayne Gunn.

Mary S, Alex K, and Sebi W, the Wednesday writing group, thanks for suggestions and feedback.

E.U. Ryan, thank you for getting me started on reading the stories of Douglas Bader, Ginger Lacey, Pierre Clostermann, Willy McKnight, Pat Pattle, Pauline Gower, Lilya Litvyak, Katya Budanova, George Beurling, Pappy Boyington, Jackie Cochran, Alfred Anderson, etc.

Thank you to The Canadian Aviation and Space Museum, The Alberta Aviation Museum, The Aero Space Museum of Calgary, and The Calgary Museum of the Regiments.

Paul, Matt, Natalie, Tiiu, and Jenna: thanks for all that you do at NeWest Press and Kisscut Design.

Thanks to creative writers at Nickle, Bowness, Lord Beaverbrook, Alternative, Forest Lawn, and Queen Elizabeth.

Thank you to Stephen of Sage Innovations (www.garryryan.ca).

Thank you to the people who run indepedent bookstores like Pages Books and Owl's Nest Books in Calgary.

Sharon, Karma, Luke, Ben, Meredith, Indiana and Ella. What's next?

In 2004, NeWest Press published Garry Ryan's first Detective Lane novel, *Queen's Park*. The second, *The Lucky Elephant Restaurant,* won a 2007 Lambda Literary Award. NeWest has since published four more titles in the series: *A Hummingbird Dance, Smoked, Malabarista* and *Foxed.* In 2009, Ryan was awarded Calgary's Freedom of Expression Award. In 2012 he began a second series with the historical fiction novel *Blackbirds,* also published by NeWest Press.